URDIN

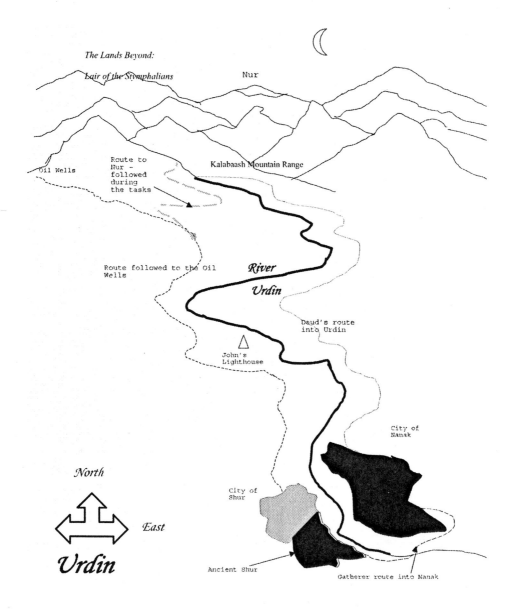

URDIN

Oz Parvaiz

iUniverse, Inc.
New York Lincoln Shanghai

Urdin

iUniverse, Inc.

For information address:
iUniverse, Inc.
2021 Pine Lake Road, Suite 100
Lincoln, NE 68512
www.iuniverse.com

ISBN: 0-595-28923-1

Printed in the United States of America

For Meena, Parvaiz, Omar, Salman and my love Adela

Nothing changes. Everything is repeated infinitely, for the pleasure of God.

—*El-Theikos*[1], Chapter 6: The Pessimists, verses 4–5

.

---

1.   Holy Scriptures

Contents

❀

Book I: In the Beginning—1007 YK

Book II: The King—1008 YK–1010 YK

Characters

❀

House of Daud:

Daud: First Judge of Nanak

Mumtaz: Daud's first wife, Jenut's mother

Helen: Daud's second wife, Zamin's mother

Jenut: Daud's older son

Zamin: Daud's younger son

Duma, Mappha, Napphish: Jenut's sons

Proteus: A descendant of Jenut, born close to a thousand years after Daud's death, Stone and Mehabiah's father

Roxanna: Proteus's wife, Stone and Mehabiah's mother

Stone: A descendant of Jenut, Proteus's older son

Mehabiah: A descendant of Jenut, Proteus's younger son

Joshua's Family:

Acrisius: Jesus, Sophia, and Joshua's father

Meena: Acrisius's wife, Jesus, Sophia, and Joshua's mother

Jesus: Acrisius's older son

Sophia: Acrisius's daughter

Joshua: Acrisius's younger son

Others:

John the Gatherer: A city politician, Joshua and Stone's mentor

Paris: A clergyman and city politician

Ahab: A clergyman, Paris's close friend

Arjuna: Stone's friend and bodyguard

Jonathan: Stone's guard

Samuel: A Gatherer

Esau: A king of Nanak, born into the line of Zamin

Nahum: A soldier

Ali: A soldier

The End: 1010 YK[1]

✿

The tower clock struck twelve. His robes were drenched. The sky shook with thunder. The streets were flooded. Tall buildings rose on each side. The cold wind slashed through his wet robes and brought tears to his eyes.

He kept walking.

They hid themselves in the shadows of a building. They were worried. He was late. They walked out into the furious storm and stared in the direction of the tower.

They stepped back into the shadows.

He was tired. The wound was deep. He kept walking. Lightning had struck a building. He stopped. A child stood before him. The child pointed at him, turned around and ran into a nearby alley. He followed the child into the darkness.

---

1. The Year of Kings marked by the coronation of Zamin in 00YK

The two men waited patiently. He had told them not to move. They had argued with him the day before. "Bring someone with you." "No, I'll meet you there." "Bring someone with you." "Don't worry." "What if…?" "Don't worry."

He stood in the alley. The child had disappeared.
An old wrinkled hand reached out to him from within the darkness.
"Come, walk toward me," the old man said.
He walked deeper into the alley.
"Who's there?" he asked.
"Is it you?" the old man asked.
He stopped. He pondered the question.
"Welcome home," the old man said.
"I know who you are," he said.
"Of course you do," the old man replied.
Lightning flashed across the sky. There were nine men in the alley. The old man was crouched in front of them, his hands still reaching out to him.
"What do you want?" he asked.

"Do you see him?" the second man asked.
"No," the first man replied.
The first man was worried.
"Where is he?"
"This isn't like him."
"You're right, let's go."
"No," the first man said. "Be patient."
They waited for a while and then the first man walked out into the street.
"His wound hasn't healed yet," the first man said. "He said he'd come from the east, past the tower clock."
"Are you sure?"
"Yes."
The second man nodded. They started running.

The nine men carried a white cloth. He didn't move. Lightning flashed again. They stood around him. He closed his eyes and looked up at the sky. The cold rain fell on his face. They wrapped the cloth tightly around his body.

They ran desperately down the street. He was never late. "Where was he?" They looked into each alley as they ran by. They slipped and fell, but they kept running. Why had they waited so long?

The first knife tore through his abdomen. A gush of blood stained the white cloth. Air quickly escaped his lungs. He opened his eyes, but he could see nothing. A purple haze absorbed the world around him. He couldn't breathe. His hands were covered with blood. He could taste it on his lips. He fell to his knees. "Were you chosen?" the old man asked, as the last dagger pierced his heart.

The two men heard the thunder and saw the lightning. They prayed for him. They loved him. They kept running. They were tired. They ran faster. They turned into an alley. They found him. His body was tightly wrapped in a crimson cloth. His lifeless eyes stared blankly at the sky, and a trail of blood flowed away from his body into a nearby drain.

Book I:
In the Beginning—1007 YK

＊

Jenut and Zamin

On that day when God's opponents gathered together they were driven into the fire. And over a few ill-omened moments, He destroyed the heavens and the earth. He let loose on them a howling gale, and they felt the wrath and punishment of sin. Now the earth was indescribable and vacuous, darkness was over her, and the spirit of God was no longer.

—*El-Theikos*, Chapter 1: Advent, verses 1–3

Mehabiah looked out at the river. The bridge loomed above him. The water was black.

"Any sign of them?" Samuel whispered from behind.

"No," Mehabiah said.

"The longer they take the more they'll have," Samuel said.

"Is everything ready?" Mehabiah asked.

"Yes."

"They'll be tired," Mehabiah said.

"Can I go next time?"

"I don't know," Mehabiah replied. "You'll have to ask him."

"I think I see them," Samuel said.

The water moved. Ripples grasped the shore. A huge raft silently appeared from within the thick fog. Five men steered the raft. They skillfully directed it toward the riverbank. Mehabiah stepped forward and held out his hand.

"Joshua," Mehabiah said.

"Yes," one of the five raftsmen replied, as he held Mehabiah's hand and climbed ashore.

"How's Nanak?" Mehabiah asked.

Joshua shrugged his shoulders.

"Is your brother still in the mountains?" Joshua asked.

"Yes."

"He should stop going."

"He'll be fine," Mehabiah said.

"I'm sure he will."

"Welcome back to Shur, Joshua," Mehabiah said.

Joshua held Mehabiah's hand and smiled.

"We should go to the festival before it ends," Joshua said.

The men unloaded the raft and carried the luggage to a nearby building.

❧   ❧   ❧

Not far away, in the old section of Shur, the annual festival was winding down. A large group of people had congregated around John the Gatherer. He was an old man with a sharp wit and a talent for storytelling. He supported himself with a crude cane. His hair was thin and his face was round.

As he spoke he looked at the people through his beady blue eyes and smiled. Softly, in almost a whisper, his voice traveled slowly out toward the crowd, pulling everyone in, even closer to him. He had just begun his story when Mehabiah and Joshua arrived. People turned and greeted the two men.

"How was the Gathering, Joshua?" John asked.

"Good," replied Joshua. "And how are you?"

"Fine," said John. "I'm retelling the history of Daud and the caravans. Do you want me to start over?"

"That's quite all right, John," said Joshua. "Please continue."

Joshua looked around him. Everyone had their eyes fixed on him. He smiled at as many people as he could.

Everyone stood in a circle around the old storyteller. Joshua was happy to be back in Shur. He could relax for a few days. He turned his attention to John and the history of his ancestors—the history of Shur.

"...and then the prophets looked to God," John said lifting his head up toward the sky, "but He did not answer them. They prayed and they built temples, but God would not speak.

"Life on earth was ravaged, and the fruitless trees gave no shelter. The rivers boiled turbid with mud in vast eddies whose seething flood poured sand into the streams. A dark shroud coated the heavens, and a gray layer of ashy silt carpeted the earth. There were no meadows, no deserts, only stretches of black ash, blown around by a dull, warm, unnatural wind. Many perished in the arms of the black new world that had snatched man from Gae's breast and plunged him into bitter death.

"As the years passed, man traveled in caravans, floating aimlessly, from one destination to another in search of pure land, but there was none. Year after year, the migration continued, and gradually, man learned new ways to eat, to live, to survive.

"But the prophets didn't forget God. They prepared sacraments in His honor for centuries after the destruction. They worshipped and preached God's message from the remnants of the Old World, and they prayed for divine guidance.

"And then, three hundred years before the reign of Esau, their prayers were answered. In the mountains of Kalabaash, at the foot of Mount Nur, across the great plains of the river Urdin, God broke his silence. On that night, a tremendous blast awoke the people to a blinding light, which devoured Mount Nur. The people followed the light into a small cave, and from within the cave a voice addressed the people: 'Bring me the man they call Daud.'

"So the people found Daud, and he followed the light into the cave. There, God spoke to him: 'These are your people. Lead them through the mountains into the plains that surround the river Urdin. And there you will dwell. You are blessed, and I will bless those who bless you and curse those who curse you.'

"So Daud led his people through the treacherous mountains, into the plains of the river Urdin. And there on the east side of the river, he discovered the oasis city of Nanak, and on the west side he discovered the city of Havilah Shur. After finding no sign of inhabitants, Daud assumed that the natives had fled during the days of the destruction. He thus claimed the cities for his people.

"The buildings in Nanak were better suited for the caravan. So Daud blessed Nanak as their home. In the city, Daud and his followers found great libraries with books from the ancient world—texts composed by Aristotle, Aquinas, Khyam, Camus and many others. In the meantime, Shur, which lay across the river connected to Nanak by a great bridge, remained abandoned.

"On the day of the settlement the Elders in Nanak wrote songs praising the Lord, proclaiming the city holy. At night the people united in joyous celebration, temporarily erasing the past with Pan-like revelry. They didn't have to breathe the air of the treacherous lands beyond the Kalabaash anymore." John took a deep breath and cleared his voice. Everyone was sitting down now. They looked at him intently as he continued his story.

"And thus the migration came to an end.

"In the years that followed, there was peace in Nanak. A Council governed the city, and presiding over the Council was a Judge. The first Judge of Nanak was Daud. Daud was seventy years old when he was made Judge of Nanak. He ruled wisely for many years and the people were happy. But their worries grew in proportion to Daud's wrinkles.

"Since the settlement, the Council members had moved in the direction of Iblis's lair. Corruption was rampant, and the citizens worried about the future of Nanak. Soon enough, the people came to Daud and asked for a king. They wanted a chosen successor. But Daud was not pleased. He told the people of Nanak what a king would do: 'He will take your sons and make them serve his household. His ambition will thwart your sanctity. He will take the best of your land, and you yourselves will become his slaves, and when that day comes, you will cry for relief from the king you have chosen. So look toward God, who will always be your king.' Daud also convinced the people that he would put an end to the corruption. The people trusted him, and so they turned around and returned to their homes.

"But Daud had no real answers and he needed guidance. As chronicled in *El-Theikos*, during his time of need, God came to Daud in a dream. In the dream, Daud saw himself as a pigeon perched on a mountaintop. God sat beside him. Before them, thousands of men walked toward a rainbow. And above them flew a multitude of pigeons that directed the men toward the rainbow.

"The next morning, Daud spoke to an oracle about his dream. The oracle said, 'Your children will be the messengers of God, and they will lead the people of Nanak to solidarity.' But Daud laughed. He doubted his vision. He doubted God, because he had no children, and he was an old man. But the oracle assured Daud to have faith in his vision, because 'God speaks clearly and truly'.

"And sure enough, thirty years after the first settlement, God brought joy to Daud's household. His wife, Mumtaz, bore him his first son. However, the happiness was short-lived. Mumtaz died hours after giving life to her child.

The boy was named Jenut, and despite the grief that accompanied Mumtaz's death, the Nanakites were relieved that the house of Daud finally had an heir.

"Soon after, according to custom, Daud married Mumtaz's sister Helen. Helen, who couldn't have children of her own, happily took on her sister's role as mother and wife. Daud and Helen lived happily. She brought peace to Daud's household and he loved her dearly. At this time, only the oracle and Helen knew of Daud's vision.

"A few years later, during a particularly cold winter, a miracle fell upon Daud's house. Helen, in the twilight of her life, bore him a son, whom he called Zamin. Daud's happiness had multiplied. The thirteen-year-old Jenut celebrated the miracle extravagantly and prepared a great feast in honor of his younger brother. Everyone in the city attended the feast. Even though the feast was for Zamin, the people gravitated toward the charismatic Jenut. During Zamin's introduction, Jenut lifted his brother into the air and kissed his forehead, as the people broke out into a cheer on his behalf. Helen was not pleased with the attention her stepson regularly received from the Council and from the citizen's of Nanak. Moreover, she detested being the mother of Daud's second-born child.

"Seven years after Zamin's birth, Helen spoke before a Council meeting and claimed that Zamin was God's gift to Daud. He was a miracle child. She also spoke of Daud's vision and claimed that Zamin was the rightful heir of Nanak.

"In the streets of Nanak, the rumors of Daud's vision spread rapidly and the people grew restless once again. The people trusted Daud, but detested everyone else on the Council. Thus the citizens of Nanak gathered together once more and came to Daud. They said to him, 'You are old, and the Council does not walk in your ways; now appoint a king from the house of Daud, so that he can lead us like the nations of the past and like the birds in your vision.' Daud tried once again to convince the people that a king would suppress them, but they would not listen. A judge was not sufficient anymore. So Daud promised the people that he would appoint a king.

"As Daud leaned toward appointing Jenut king, tensions in his household and in Nanak grew. Helen and the elder Councilmen were convinced that Zamin was a divine miracle, and they threatened a coup d'état in the name of God. They came to Daud and said 'Get rid of your son, for he shall never share an inheritance with Zamin.' Dejected by the actions of his wife and clergy, Daud slipped into a deep depression.

"Jenut saw his father's sadness, and approached Daud, asking for his leave. In order to restore peace to Nanak, Jenut would search for a kingdom in the lands beyond. Daud was furious and turned down Jenut's request. But Jenut persisted with his argument. Father and son spoke for many days, and finally Jenut convinced his father that his departure was for the best. With tears in his eyes, Daud told his son that he could leave on one condition: He would have to eventually return. On that day, Jenut and Daud formed a covenant in which the son promised the father that he would return to dwell in Nanak and die on holy land. After the covenant, Jenut gathered a few men and left the city. On his way out thousands of Nanakites followed him across the bridge, toward the mountains and into the lands beyond.

"Soon after, in 00 YK, Daud anointed Zamin as the first king of Nanak. That day, the people of Nanak came to Zamin's court and asked him questions about justice and government. Zamin's answers did not satisfy the people. They stormed out of his court and sent a messenger in search of Jenut. Refusing to return immediately, Jenut assured the Nanakite messenger that he would visit his father's temple once a year.

"Between 00YK and 44YK, Jenut and his followers traveled through the ashes, returning every year to Nanak for food and for worship. And every year, his brother Zamin refused to see him. Eventually, however, Jenut's followers grew restless and asked if they could return and live in Nanak again. Jenut was old and he remembered his father's covenant. So he led his people back through the mountains, toward the holy city.

"Back in Nanak, Zamin grew weary at word of his brother's return. So he placed an army of men around the city walls and commanded them to destroy Jenut's caravan. As soon as Jenut closed in on the city gates, the army charged his followers. Unarmed and helpless, they fled over the bridge toward the city of Shur. Zamin's soldiers pursued, but the bridge was not strong enough, and it collapsed. Most of Jenut's caravan reached the other side, but many drowned. Zamin, too, lost more than half his cavalry to the raging river.

"Over the next few weeks Jenut sent messengers across Urdin begging for food, but Zamin shunned their requests. Jenut's people were starving, but God was with them. The strongest and ablest men in Shur banded together and crossed the river Urdin into Nanak, and they brought back food for their brothers. Jenut called these men his Gatherers, and every few months they were sent into Nanak scrounging for anything they could lay their hands on.

"In the meantime, Jenut's people took refuge in the deserted buildings of Havilah Shur. As the years passed their refuge eventually became their home—our home.

"Jenut died in the year 56 YK. He could see the city of Nanak from his deathbed, and as his last breath escaped him, his sons Duma, Mappha, and Napphish promised him that one day they would return to Nanak and take what was rightfully theirs."

❧   ❧   ❧

Stone, born of Proteus in the house of Jenut one thousand years after the first settlement, had taken a caravan to the mountains to retrieve the annual supply of oil for the city of Shur. A few days after leaving the city, the caravan split into two groups. Arjuna, a renowned city soldier and Stone's close friend had taken one caravan to Mount Nur. Stone led his men west away from the river, while Arjuna headed east.

"Can you see anything?" Jonathan whispered.

Nahum turned around. "It's clear."

Jonathan and five other members of Stone's caravan crawled from behind a rock and quietly approached Nahum.

"Should we give the signal?" Jonathan asked Nahum.

"No, let's wait," Nahum replied.

"The mountains look beautiful," Jonathan said.

"They do," Nahum said.

"It's perfect. He picked the perfect night."

Nahum nodded his head.

The great mountains of Kalabaash devoured the skyline. They rose magnificently before the men. The dry plains lay behind them, stretching for miles until in the distance one could only see a glimmer of Nanak and Shur. The river divided the dry desert plains, moving silently away from the mountains toward the two cities.

"Give the signal," Nahum said.

Jonathan lit a small fire and pulled a ball of string out of his pocket. The string was drenched in oil. He lit the ball and then tossed it into the sky. It propelled down the foothills of Kalabaash.

"They'll probably join us in a while."

The men waited silently. They were dressed in white. Turbans covered their heads, and their hands and faces were caked with mud.

"Nahum?"

"Yes?"

"Do you think Joshua has returned from Nanak?" Jonathan asked.

"I'm sure he has," Nahum said.

"And the festival is probably over?" Jonathan asked.

"Yes."

"I haven't been to a festival in five years," Jonathan said. "The old part of Shur scares me."

Nahum nodded his head.

"I wish I could go to Nanak," Jonathan said.

"Joshua knows Nanak like the back of his hand."

"Joshua knows most things like the back of his hand."

"Nanak's beautiful," Nahum said. "They used the rocks from Kalabaash to rebuild the city. Joshua says that it reminds him of pictures he once saw in a book. Pictures of Rome."

"Rome," sighed Jonathan.

"It must be beautiful," Nahum said.

"What's taking them so long?" Jonathan asked.

"They're carrying oil drums."

"It never takes me so long."

"Wait!" Nahum said. "I think I hear something."

"Is it them?" Jonathan asked.

"I can't see."

"Whistle the signal."

"No," Nahum said.

"Come on, whistle it!"

"What if it's not them?"

"They'll think it's a bird."

"No!"

Despite Nahum's protest, Jonathan whistled. His whistle was returned. It echoed off of the cliffs.

"A bird in the mountains," Nahum scowled.

"What?"

"There are no birds in these mountains."

"How were we supposed to know if it was them?"

"We could have waited."

"Don't tell me…"

"Who's there?" a voice interrupted Jonathan. The men who had returned the signal had arrived.

"We are," Nahum replied.

"Is that you, Nahum?"

"Yes."

"Is Jonathan with you?"

"He's here," Nahum replied.

"And Stone?"

"He went the other way. He wanted us to wait for you."

"Good. Help us carry the drums. We'll get there faster."

Nahum and Jonathan helped the men carry the drums up the slopes of the mountain. They climbed for a while.

"Is that the cave?" Jonathan asked.

"Yes. It leads to the other side," Nahum replied.

The men walked into the cave. Darkness enveloped them. They walked a few hundred yards, after which they could see a pale blue light streaming into the tunnel. They approached the light and found themselves exiting the tunnel on the other side of Mount Tourais. A natural bridge stood before them, connecting one cliff to another. A small tributary of Urdin flowed through the ravine below. The men walked over the bridge and continued to follow the path as it descended into the ravine. Once they reached the bottom the men stopped and waited.

"It's Stone," Jonathan pointed into the distance.

Stone approached the men. They crowded around him. They felt safe. He directed the men toward the oil wells. They refilled the drums and rested for a while, waiting for the moon to commence its descent, after which they began their journey back into the warmth of Havilah Shur.

CHAPTER 2

❀

Joshua and Stone

*Then I saw a new heaven and a new earth, for the first heaven
and the first earth had passed away, and I saw a Holy City coming down from the heavens, prepared by God for His people.*

—*El-Theikos*, Chapter 15: Covenants, verse 21

"Where is it now?" Joshua asked.

"No one knows," the priest answered.

"Does it still exist?"

"According to the scriptures, 'Man sinned and God forced him to travel the
ravaged earth, never to see the beauty of the Old World again.'"

Joshua was surrounded by the high ceilings and the decorated pillars of
Jenut's temple. Everything he said and every breath he took echoed off the
walls back into the emptiness, shuffling around with other sounds, finally disappearing into a black hole of silence.

"'...and the Old World was filled with temples and streets of gold, and men
could fly like God.'"

"It must have been grand," Joshua said.

"You've seen the books and the pictures."

Joshua nodded his head and smiled. He walked away from the priest toward
a large window, which stretched from the floor to the ceiling. The sunlight,
which flowed through the window into the great hall, made Joshua's long

brown hair seem almost golden. He could see scattered clouds in the distance over the Kalabaash Mountains. The river glowed like a silver ribbon as it disappeared into the bright bloom of the evening sun.

"Are you ready for the sermon?" the priest asked.

"Yes, father," he said.

"Come to the altar, my son."

Joshua walked toward the altar and knelt before a statue of Jenut. The priest smiled at Joshua and began chanting a sermon in an ancient language.

Joshua didn't like visiting the temples and he usually avoided the priests. However, the night before, his mother had asked him to pray for her sake. Joshua stared blankly at Jenut's statue. His world began melting around him as he closed his eyes and escaped into the solace of his mind. From within the darkness different images rushed at him. He let them all pass, until he saw his older brother, Jesus. His brother was smiling. Joshua was happy. The sun was blazing down, and they had been playing for hours. Their mother sat on a short stool a few feet away, keeping a close eye on the two boys. His brother was a handsome child, with soft features, and light hair. He came running toward Joshua...

"Joshua," the calm, firm voice of Stone brought Joshua back from his daydream. Joshua turned around. Stone stood under an arched doorway behind him. The priest abruptly ended the sermon. Joshua smiled at the priest and walked toward Stone.

"Are you ready?" Stone said, as the two men quietly stepped out of the temple.

❧   ❧   ❧

Joshua stopped and looked around at the new city. Construction continued around them. The buildings were beautiful. Ancient Shur—the old city—dark and foreboding loomed in the background against the crimson of the twilight sky.

"The new city looks grand," Joshua said.

"It does," Stone agreed.

"I wonder how long the old city will stand?"

Stone shrugged his shoulders.

The two men walked toward Ancient Shur into its shadows and maze-like streets. Tall buildings surrounded them. The streets were bare, and the buildings were abandoned. The air was cold.

"*I Wish I Could Dance With John Wayne*," Joshua said.

"John Wayne?" asked Stone.

"The Duke," Joshua said.

"The man with the horse?" Stone asked.

"Yes," Joshua said. "It's the title of the book I showed you."

"I didn't read it."

"The Elders would love it." Joshua said sarcastically. "Our great corrupt priests," he mumbled.

"Not in public, Joshua," Stone said curtly.

"I wish they didn't hold a majority in the Council," Joshua said. "I'm really happy with the younger Councilmen. I gave Arjuna a copy of *The Rebel*."

"Why?" Stone asked.

"It's only a book."

"You've got too many now."

"If only I had more," Joshua said. "You should visit the libraries in Nanak sometime."

"You know I can't," Stone said. "The Elders would vilify me."

"They can't," Joshua said. "They only wish they could. The people are with you."

"'Nil tam incertum nec tam inaestimabile est quam animi multitudinis,'"[1] Stone said.

"Livy?" Joshua asked with a smile.

"His *Histories*."

"You should be ashamed of yourself," Joshua said. "Reading the books of a lost sinful world."

"You wrote them," Stone said.

"I copied them."

"So, the libraries in Nanak are great?"

"Colossal," Joshua replied. "I copy one book every time I go."

"How do they not find you?" Stone asked.

"I usually sneak in late at night through the back windows. I've yet to run into anyone. Sometimes I think they let me in and stay out of my way."

Joshua grinned and looked up at the dark sky.

"It's so grim," Joshua said.

"The last few nights have been like this."

"What's the meeting about?"

---

1.   Nothing is so uncertain or so worthless as the judgments of the mob.

"Mehabiah didn't say," said Stone. "It's probably an update on the Gathering. But I'm not sure. How was it?"

"We brought back a few things," Joshua replied. "They've invented a compass that works. Some of the Gatherers were able to bring it back for us to look at. And we collected a few books from their libraries."

"Be careful with them, Joshua."

"How were the oil wells?" asked Joshua, ignoring Stone's comment about the books.

"They're fine. Almost like clockwork," Stone replied. "I'm not sure if I need to go anymore."

"You probably shouldn't," Joshua said.

"This time it was important," Stone said. "Arjuna was heading into the mountains."

"Have you heard from him?"

"Not yet," Stone replied. "We left the city together and then parted ways."

"Does he think he'll find anything?"

"The Elders think he will," Stone said.

"I hope he's safe," Joshua said.

"The mountains are beautiful when the moon is out."

"I'm sure."

"I wish John's lighthouse worked," Stone said. "It would really help on the way back."

"He keeps a fire going sometimes," Joshua said. "And sometimes he forgets. He's getting old."

"We should spend more time with him," Stone said. "Maybe we can all have dinner together. My mother has been talking about cooking dinner for everyone. I'll speak to her and let you know."

"I spoke to your mother last night," Joshua said.

"You did?"

"We discussed the Elders," Joshua said. "She wants me to be patient."

"As we all should," Stone said. "We'll worry about the Elders when the time is right."

"How's your brother?" Joshua asked.

"He's doing well," Stone replied. "Mehabiah's a strong man."

"What does he think about the Elders?"

"He doesn't particularly like them."

"Good."

CHAPTER 3

❀

The Expedition

I went to Khuda, and after staying there three days I set out with a few men. I had not told anyone what my God had put in my heart. By night I went through the valley between the mountains of Khuda and Khabish, and to Nur, and in Nur I came upon the cave. And I stayed within Nur for seven days. And in Nur, the silence testified that 'He will be coming soon'...And if anyone takes words away from this book of prophesy, he will be punished, because our king of virtue will be coming soon.

—*El-Theikos*, Chapter 8: Jenut, verses 34–37

It is said that just before we are born, a cavern angel puts its finger to our lips and says, "Hush, don't tell what you know." This is why we have a cleft on our upper lip, and we enter our world remembering nothing of the nine choirs that encircle the throne of God.

Arjuna licked the cleft of his upper lip as he grasped for air with each swallow. The afternoon sun created a dazzling red glare. The sweat from his brow trickled into his eyes, creating a spectrum of blinding light. He rubbed his arm across his face, which only added more sweat to his eyes. He stopped.

"Ali!" he called out.

"Yes," a man behind him replied.

"I'm having trouble seeing," he said. "Let's stop for a while."

Ali waved his hand, signaling the men behind him to stop.

Arjuna stood motionless. The mountains peaked over him. The blue sky layered the heavens above, and the sun created divine patterns against the water that ran in the gorge alongside the trail. He was only fifty yards away from the valley, which led to Mount Nur.

Arjuna closed his eyes. His world turned bright red, and he could once again feel the throbbing pulse piercing against his head. He leaned over and pulled out his flask and drained water over his face. A sudden peace descended upon him. He opened his eyes and felt as if he had awoken from a deep slumber. Shades of blue coated his world as his eyes gradually refocused. He could see the small valley. He descended the steep rocks, planting his feet carefully. He gritted his teeth as he pushed down against the rocks, swiftly moving along the sharp incline into the enclave surrounded by the towering mountains.

Arjuna had grown up climbing these mountains. He had explored and mapped the Kalabaash range since he was six years old. He had accompanied his father Luke on the monthly trips to the oil wells alongside the great warrior, Proteus, Stone's father. After Proteus's death, the trips continued with Stone and Arjuna. Therefore, when the Council sent out an expedition in search of the final lost scriptures of Daud, Arjuna had been appointed to lead the mission. He felt proud that Stone had trusted him with the city's future. They had embraced only a few days earlier at the foothills of Kalabaash. Arjuna continued his journey east toward Mount Nur, parting ways with Stone who proceeded west toward the oil wells.

The small valley leading to Mount Nur was strangely cooler than the rest of the mountain range. He looked up at the sky and smiled. He turned around.

"The rest of you stay here," Arjuna said to the men behind him.

He continued walking. The blue mountain with a coat of ice and snow was Nur. It stood out against the surrounding bare, brown mountains. Arjuna walked toward Nur, knowing that he would be at its base by sunset. He walked through the thorn bushes, removing all obstacles with a small axe. Once through the thicket, Arjuna located the cave. "The scriptures will be a mile in," the Elders had told him. He covered his face and pulled out his dagger. He then walked into the darkness, which swallowed him completely.

As he walked deeper into the cave, Arjuna thought of the cavern angel and the hidden truth. Deep in his heart, he hoped that he would find the scriptures. If he did, he felt his faith in God would be reaffirmed. Throughout his young life, Arjuna had listened and faithfully followed God. He knew that he had to believe because his priests had told him that a life without God was lived in despair. He often spoke with Joshua. Joshua, he suspected, was an atheist. But Joshua was not in despair.

The Elders had been searching for years until they finally pieced together the numerous clues scattered within *El-Theikos*, pointing them to Nur and the lost scriptures. He had memorized their directions. Arjuna was only a few yards away from the holy text, which had been misplaced in 250 YK. He bent down and lifted a rock and dropped it to his aside. The sound of the stone hitting the ground echoed off of the cave walls. He moved a few more stones aside and found a wooden case. He lifted it and placed it beside him. He opened it. The manuscript lay in the case. He put the manuscript in a bag and walked back toward the mouth of the cave.

As he slowly walked out of the cave, Arjuna realized that he felt nothing. He had just found the lost scriptures of *El-Theikos* and yet he felt nothing. No feelings of divinity or grandeur overcame him. All he felt was all he knew: his sensations. He was in a dark cave, with a cool breeze, walking alongside a cave wall, holding a heavy manuscript. Maybe he had thought about the moment for so long that the anticipation had dwindled the enthusiasm, or maybe he was too tired to feel anything. He knew that he wanted to get back to camp and sleep. He wished that he wasn't so tired. He wished that he could feel something more than just the desire to return to his entourage and lay down.

CHAPTER 4.

❀

Believer

These are the revelations of a wise book, a guidance and blessing to the righteous, who attend to their prayers and believe in the fruits of eternal bliss. They are the blessed, who are rightly guided by their lord, and through His glory they will surely prosper and those who disbelieve, whether you forewarn them or not they will not have faith. God has set a seal upon their hearts; their sight is dimmed and grievous punishments await them.

—El-Theikos, Chapter 6: The Believers, verses 1–4

The ball rolled across the pavement. The children ran after it. They wrestled for it. A child with light hair rose victoriously from the pile. He lifted the ball into the air. He smiled giddily. The other boys tried to snatch the ball from him, but he held it close to his chest and struggled against them. The struggle continued. He kept smiling.

The sun blazed down furiously. The pavement was smoldering, but the children barely noticed. Their attention was focused on the ball. Joshua sat across the street and smiled at the children. The game reminded him of his brother when they were younger. He could see *his brother playing across the street, running away from the hoard of children with the ball tucked away carefully under his right arm. He could see himself chasing after the ball. He could see himself tripping and scraping his knee. His brother stopped and turned around.*

The game was over. Joshua was injured. He held his knee and cried. His brother came up to him and gave him the ball. He stopped crying. But the crying did not stop. The children across the street were still playing. One of them was bawling. He had just tripped. The young boy with light hair stopped running and the children stopped playing. They looked around for help. They spotted Joshua, and they waved.

Joshua waved back and asked them if they needed help. They all nodded and Joshua walked across the street toward them. The child stopped crying when he saw Joshua approach him. He was only five, but he didn't want Joshua to see him cry. Blood flowed down his knee.

"That's not good," Joshua said, kneeling down.

"I fell," the child replied.

"My sister lives next door. Let's see if she can help."

Joshua carried the child to his sister's house. The children followed him.

"How was the Gathering, Joshua?" the boy with light hair asked.

"Good," Joshua replied.

"Is it dangerous?"

"Yes."

"Do you swim to Nanak?"

"No, I go on a raft."

"Do you swim through the tunnels?"

"Yes," Joshua replied. "The raft doesn't take me all the way."

"Who's going with you next time?"

"A few new people."

"Can I go?"

"No," Joshua smiled. He was thinking of his brother again. Joshua missed him. The young boy looked like him. There was something about his smile. Everyone loved his smile. Joshua didn't like Gatherings anymore. They reminded him of his brother too much.

He stopped in front of his sister's house and knocked on the door. Sophia answered. She hugged Joshua and carried the child inside. The rest of the children waited outside.

Joshua walked into his sister's house. He liked the dark hallways; only a little sunlight made its way through. He walked toward the courtyard. The hall smelled damp. It had rained for weeks. Joshua left the hall and walked into the sun-drenched courtyard.

Sophia's husband Mehabiah, five years her junior, was sleeping in a hammock that stretched between two apple trees. He seemed comfortable. His right leg hung outside the hammock. Joshua smiled and walked toward Mehabiah. He stood silently next to the hammock for a few minutes. Then, when he was perfectly sure that Mehabiah was indeed fast asleep, he jumped into the hammock and crushed Mehabiah beneath him. Mehabiah awoke gasping for air. He saw Joshua on top of him and laughed. They wrestled each other off the hammock onto the courtyard floor. The wrestling continued until both men realized that they didn't have enough energy to keep going. They weren't children anymore. They sat down across from each other on the two chairs in the courtyard. They smiled at each other and remained seated silently for a while. Mehabiah broke the silence.

"Warm day."

"John said it would be," Joshua said.

"He was at the meeting," Mehabiah said.

"John?" Joshua seemed surprised.

"He wanted to speak to you," Mehabiah said.

"Why?" Joshua asked.

"I don't know," Mehabiah said.

"I should've stayed longer," Joshua said.

"Why'd you storm out?" Mehabiah said.

Joshua chose not to answer him.

"I spoke on your behalf," Mehabiah said.

"What did the Elders have to say?"

"I'm Stone's younger brother," Mehabiah said. "They listened."

"How'd the vote turn out?"

"The Gatherings will continue," Mehabiah said. "But they're not happy about the books."

"Good."

"It's the books," Mehabiah said. "They want to ban Gatherings because of the books."

"I'd still go."

"They know that."

"They always separate us," said Joshua. "We entered the great hall and they stepped forward and pulled Stone away."

The two men were silent once again. Mehabiah looked at the ground. He was thinking. He was thinking about his next words. Joshua allowed him to think.

"The expedition returned."

"When?"

"This morning," Mehabiah said. "The Elders are keeping it quiet. I think Arjuna found the scriptures. I didn't think they existed. The Elders spoke about the expedition briefly. They want to meet with Stone."

"Stone was in the mountains yesterday?"

"Yes," Mehabiah said. "And he brought back oil."

"He shouldn't go to mountains." Joshua said. "It's too dangerous."

"And the Gatherings are not dangerous?" said Mehabiah.

"Five people from Shur died the last time they went for oil."

"And what about Jesus…"

"Not now, Mehabiah," Joshua interrupted.

"I'm sorry."

Mehabiah had spoken without thinking.

"Do you think the child is fine now?" Joshua changed the subject.

"Sophia!" Mehabiah called out for his wife.

She walked in. She was beautiful. Her face was soft and her skin was clear. She smiled when she looked at Joshua.

"My sweet brother," she said.

Joshua loved her dearly.

"How's the child?" Mehabiah asked.

"I let him go out and play," Sophia said. "He should be fine. He spoke about Joshua every second that I was with him. Joshua this and Joshua that. The great Joshua!"

Sophia had a twinkle in her eye as she teased her brother.

"Please bring us some water," Sophia told her husband. "Let me speak with my brother."

Mehabiah stood up and walked to the kitchen. Joshua and Sophia were left alone. She turned to make sure Mehabiah had left the courtyard.

"What is wrong with you?" Sophia said sternly to her brother.

Joshua was taken aback by his sister's comment.

"You walked out of the Council meeting?" she asked.

"Yes."

"Why?" Sophia asked. "Stone can't support you if you act like a child."

"I didn't act like a child."

"Thank God for Mehabiah," Sophia said. "He vouched for you. He begged the Council for Gatherings to continue."

"I'm tired, Sophia," Joshua said.

"Of what?"

"Of everything," he said. "Ever since I started going to Nanak."

"What difference does that make?"

"It makes a difference," Joshua said.

"You're losing your mind," Sophia said. "The Council is right to ban Gatherings."

"No they're not," Joshua said. "What does the Council know?"

"I think they should ban Gatherings."

"Have you ever read a book other than *El-Theikos*?" Joshua asked.

"No," Sophia said. "And I don't think I need to."

"How would you know?"

"Because God is with me, Joshua," Sophia said. "I don't have to search for him in ancient books."

"I'm not searching for Him," Joshua said. "I stopped searching for Him."

"You're a fool."

"When I'm on Gatherings, the saddest part is when I have to return to Shur."

"Don't say that!" Sophia said. "Mother will die. Have a heart."

"Have a heart?" Joshua repeated his sister. "You didn't see Jesus die."

"Don't bring that up again," she said. "I felt it as much as you did."

"Do you even remember what yesterday was?"

"You think everyone has forgotten."

"That's because everyone has."

"And you're the only one who remembers our brother?"

"Sometimes I feel I am," Joshua said.

"He believed in God," Sophia said emphatically.

"No, he didn't," Joshua said. "You don't remember, Sophia."

"I do remember."

"I think I should leave," Joshua said.

He stood up and walked slowly away from the courtyard into the darkness. His sister was angry. She followed him.

"Come back here and sit down!"

"I can't talk to you right now," Joshua replied.

"I'm your older sister," Sophia said. "Come back and sit down!"

Joshua turned around. He looked at Sophia. He felt like a child. Sophia stood before him like his mother used to. He didn't want to leave the house angry, and she knew it. She smiled at him.

"Come back here," she said softly.

He smiled and walked toward Sophia. She hugged him warmly. He didn't like arguing with her.

"I just want you to be careful," she said. "Your ideas."

"I'm sorry if I said anything that hurt you."

"You know that I loved our brother as much as you did," Sophia said. "I wasn't there when he died. It probably kills you every time you think about it. But he's still with us. He'll always be with us."

"No, Sophia," Joshua said. "He left us a long time ago."

❧   ❧   ❧

Smoke rose to the top of the temple. An old man in white robes walked slowly to the altar. He was followed closely by four priests. The rest of the clergy lined up against the walls. The old man stopped and knelt down in front of a statue of Jenut. The clergy began chanting hymns in the background. The sweet, melodic sounds filled the massive temple.

The old man looked up at Jenut's statue. He closed his eyes. Tears streamed down his face. He had been a servant of God and a member of the guild of priests since he was fifteen, but he knew that Shur was slowly moving away from religious doctrine.

He stood up and turned around, his back now facing the statue. He looked at the sea of Elders before him. Their wrinkled faces bowed down, deep in meditation. He bowed his head and opened a small door in the back of his mind, entering it carefully, disappearing into another consciousness void of earthly elements, where thought dictates all laws. He visualized God and he felt peace. "You are not alone, Paris," He said.

But Paris felt sad. He felt lost. He feared that God would slip away from Shur. Unbeknownst to others, he had read the books of the old world, and he feared that a second plague would result from the moral bankruptcy, spiritual dissolution, and deceptive illusions that were accompanying Joshua's secret attempts to re-enlighten the community.

For a thousand years religion had played a pivotal role in the development of the city, and the people of Shur had been content. They had found their spiritual answers in God, and they had found an earthly refuge in the temple.

During the early days of Shur, soon after the expulsion, the Shurites had been obsessed with thoughts of returning to Nanak. But the Elders had comforted them with the knowledge that God was always with them, and the Promised Land across Urdin would be delivered to them if they demonstrated true faith.

The people's religious faith had naturally also translated into political trust, as most of the elected Councilmen were clergy members. The legislature itself was patterned after religious doctrine, and initially only members of Jenut's household and priests served on the City Council. As a child, he remembered the absolute faith people had demonstrated in the religion of Jenut and the ways of the Elders.

Then, in 955 YK, John the Gatherer entered political life and ruined everything.

CHAPTER 5

✿

The Lost Scriptures

O mankind! Verily there hath come to you a convincing proof from your Lord. For we have sent unto you a light.

—*El-Theikos*, Chapter 10: Prophesies, verses 2–4

The water was cold. Joshua held his breath and plunged beneath the waves. Wild reeds flowed with the currents of the river. He pushed the water away from him and moved into the dark depths of Urdin. Beneath the waves in the distance he saw a light. Around the light was a garden. In the center of the garden was a sundial. Joshua smiled. Next to the sundial he saw a tall man. He swam toward the man. He felt confused. He recognized the man before him. He became sad. His head started throbbing. He shut his eyes.

"Open your eyes," the man said.

Joshua knew the voice.

"You're dead!" Joshua replied.

"Open your eyes."

"No!" Joshua said again. "You're dead."

"Open your eyes."

He gripped Joshua's shoulders and shook him.

"No!"

"Open your eyes."

"No."

"Wake up."

"Come on, Joshua. Wake up!"

He opened his eyes. It was dark. He lay on his bed. He was sweating. His mother stood over him.

"You must wake up!"

"What's wrong?"

"There's a riot," his mother said. "Look outside."

Joshua walked toward the window. Thousands of people were scrambling toward the Capitol in a chaotic frenzy. Joshua rubbed his eyes and tried to shake away the lingering dream. He turned around and walked toward the wooden closet next to his bed. His mother seemed disturbed.

"What are you doing?" asked his mother.

"I'll change and go outside."

"Are you sure?"

"Yes, Ma."

"Take the lantern with you."

"I will."

"And be careful."

"I'll try."

"Do you want me to come with you?"

"No, Mother," he replied. "I'll be back soon."

He put on his black coat and walked toward the front door. He could hear the crowd. He opened the door. The moonlight flowed in. He stood under the doorway and looked at the mob before him. He remained calm. He walked toward the crowd and waited for a familiar face. The crowd rushed by him like a fierce river. He pulled his collar up and put his hands in his pocket. He saw someone he knew. As soon as the person was closer, Joshua grabbed his arm and pulled him out of the rabble.

"Joshua!" the man exclaimed.

"What's going on, Sinon?" Joshua asked.

"He's mentioned in the scriptures."

"What?"

"The Elders said it."

"Stone?" Joshua asked.

"Yes," Sinon replied. "The Lost Scriptures proclaim him. Paris said it in the temple."

"When?"

"A few hours ago."

"And word spread so quickly?"

"Every temple in Shur had a sermon tonight."

"Where's Stone?"

"He's at the Capitol," Sinon replied. "I think they're presenting him."

"Presenting him?"

"Yes."

"Have you seen Mehabiah?"

"No."

"And Arjuna?"

"Arjuna's at the Capitol," Sinon replied. "Are you coming, Joshua?"

"You keep going, Sinon," Joshua said. "I'll follow you there in a while."

Sinon jumped back into the crowd. Joshua looked at the faces as they passed by. Their faith astounded him. They really believed. "Illusions," he thought to himself. He could hear the magicians cry, "Miracles at the Capitol...Free Miracles at the Capitol!" His brother had seen it coming. "Don't let them take you," he had told Joshua. And Joshua had listened. He found Jesus's diary that night and read it. He absorbed his brother's soul. It was natural. Someone had to keep him alive.

His sister had forgotten. His mother had stopped talking. Their house had been silent for years. The warmth had died. During his saddest moments, Joshua would think about Jesus, and he would feel depressingly lonely. He would stay awake late into the night, his agony gouging at what remained of his heart, like vultures upon a carcass, until there was an empty, gaping hole in his chest. And then he would listen for it quietly and hope that his heart was there no longer. After a few moments of silence and complete peace, he'd finally slip into a deep slumber. He'd have nightmares. He would wake up in pain. He would feel the ghastly rhythm within his chest again—the monotonous, unoriginal repetition.

He walked quietly amongst the crowd. He looked at the people around him. Poor souls. Did they know? Did they know about God? Did they know about his brother? His death? How could they? They were too busy building castles in heaven. Too busy to live. "Go to bed," he felt like telling them. But he didn't. He just walked quietly along.

They were closer to the Capitol. He could see the white dome rise into the sky. He squinted his eyes and looked for Stone.

"Joshua!" a man shouted.

Joshua turned around.

"Mehabiah," Joshua replied.

"My brother's looking for you."

"Where is he?"

"Follow me."

Mehabiah entered the building from a side door. They walked through long, winding hallways until they reached the main chamber. The chamber was crowded with Councilmen. Stone stood between John and Councilman Paris. Joshua approached the three men. Stone stepped forward and embraced Joshua.

"I'm glad Mehabiah found you," Stone said.

"I was asleep," Joshua replied.

"Joshua, wait out here for a while," Stone said. "John wants to talk to me."

"Joshua, son," John said. "I wish to speak with you separately as well."

Joshua smiled at John and nodded his head.

John and Stone left the congregation of men and walked into a room adjacent to the main chamber. John had been Stone's mentor ever since he was a child. Stone always felt comfortable discussing matters of importance with him. Stone closed the door behind him. The room was silent. John was waiting for Stone to speak. Stone sat down and John followed suit.

"They found the lost scriptures," Stone said.

"I heard."

"I've been looking for you all day."

"Have you spoken to Mehabiah?" John asked.

"Yes," Stone replied.

"Do the scriptures mention you?"

"They speak of the holy cave, Nur and a king...chosen from the house of Jenut.'"

"You?" John asked.

"The Elders think so."

"Why you?" John asked.

"The prophecy places this king in the eleventh century," Stone said.

"And?"

"He's supposed to complete three tasks chosen by God before he's recognized. 'And he will lead his men into the mountains for refuge, returning to Shur victorious.' Three tasks."

"What kind of tasks?" John asked.

"We're not sure yet," Stone replied.

"Are you going to do them?" John asked.

"You would expect me to."

"What about Mehabiah?" John asked.

"What about him?"

"He's a son of Jenut," John said. "Maybe the scriptures speak of him."

"He's a child," Stone said.

"He's twenty-eight."

"It's not him," Stone said.

"How do you know?"

"The Elders have said that it's not him."

"How do they know?"

"They're studying the scriptures right now."

"Why aren't you in there with them?" John asked.

"Only holy men are allowed inside," Stone replied.

"You've been anointed by God, and you're not holy?"

"Not yet."

"Can I see them?"

"I'm not sure if you can."

"Whether I can or not, can you work out a way for me to see them?"

"I can try."

The two men were silent. John looked up at the ceiling. He was thinking deeply.

"Why now?" John asked.

"I've been asking myself the same question."

"Why did they find the scriptures now?" John mumbled softly to himself.

"A miracle," Stone replied.

"You can't afford to believe in miracles."

Stone nodded his head in agreement.

"Paris knows that you and Joshua are going to make a push toward secular government," John said.

"He cannot," Stone replied. "We haven't told anyone."

"He suspects it then," said John. "After one thousand years, the religious grip of the clergy is slipping away."

"He's afraid," Stone said.

"How does Paris prevent it?"

"He makes himself more powerful," Stone said.

"He anoints his enemy," John said. "Can one remove the power that anoints him?"

"…without himself losing religious legitimacy?" Stone completed John's question.

"If that's the case, he's smarter than I thought," John said. "But then, this may be real. God's plan. After all, your grandfathers were prophets."

"If I am the chosen one, then the tasks should be simple."

"You'll become king," John said. "And the Elders will be your clergy. But then how do we get rid of them?"

"We should speak with Joshua."

"Just kill them," John said.

Stone laughed.

"You need to find out about the tasks," John said.

"Mehabiah is looking into it."

"Keep Joshua close to you."

"I know."

"When are you leaving for the tasks?"

"In a few days," Stone said. "We have to travel to Kalabaash. I'll put together a caravan."

"Take the Elders with you," John said. "Keep them outside the city."

"I should leave Joshua in Shur?"

"I think that's wise," John said. "He'll protect the city for you. Leave the army with him. He's popular with the army."

"And Mehabiah?"

"Keep Mehabiah with you," John replied. "And at least one legion of trusted soldiers."

"We'll be all right."

"Are you still sharp with the sword?"

"Yes."

"Keep practicing with Joshua," John said.

"I will."

"Speak to him, and make him comfortable about the future," John said.

"I will."

"Am I forgetting anything?"

"Everything will work out fine."

"Indeed," John said softly, his blue eyes gleaming with assurance.

❧   ❧   ❧

"Dark clouds," Paris said pointing out toward the black sky.

"We need rain," Zia replied.

"The river will flow over," said Ahab.

"We have the dams in place," said Paris.

"How's Joshua?" asked Ahab.

"He's calmed down," replied Zia.

"He used to be such a nice child," Paris said. "I never thought he'd be a problem. Jesus maybe, but never Joshua."

"He'll be fine," said Ahab.

"He's very angry," said Zia.

"He thinks too much," said Paris.

"Does he still believe?" asked Ahab.

"No," said Zia.

"And the Gatherers?" asked Paris.

"They'll die for him," said Ahab.

"How many are there?" asked Paris.

"About one hundred," replied Ahab. "They're 'silent.' They don't reveal their identities. Except for Joshua, because of the Council seat."

"You're not a Gatherer, are you?" Paris smiled.

"No," Ahab replied.

The three Elders stood on the balcony and saw the sun set before them. The sky was scarred with the red rays of twilight. A younger man walked onto the balcony.

"Councilman Stone asks for Councilman Zia," he said.

Zia paid his respects to Ahab and Paris and stepped off the balcony. Paris and Ahab remained on the balcony. They were the oldest Councilmen.

"We're losing," Paris said. "For the first time in a thousand years, we're losing."

"The scriptures will help."

"What did Stone say?"

"He's still thinking."

"Miracles."

"No man can refuse being anointed by God," Ahab said. "How long do you think he'll take?"

"He'll speak to John," said Paris. "It'll all work out."

"According to God's plan," Ahab said.

"Of course."

CHAPTER 6

❄

The Journey

The chosen son of Jenut is a man affirmed by the Creator for the house of Daud. He is the purpose and the foreknowledge of the Supreme Being, and through his miracles, wonders and signs, the Lord's divisions will march unto Nanak.

—*El-Theikos*, Chapter 15: Restoration, verses 1–2

The air was warm. Mehabiah could barely breathe. He looked around at the vast stretches of sand and then at the glaring sun, which flashed brightly in his eyes. In the distance, he could see sterile, black clouds hovering around Kalabaash—clouds with no rain and no relief. He knew that the further they traveled from Urdin the more treacherous the journey would become. Yet, the caravan moved steadily toward Mount Nur.

Stone rode at the front of the caravan. Five hundred men and camels followed him. Mehabiah galloped his camel toward Stone.

"We picked a bad day."

"We'll make it," Stone replied.

"The sun should be setting soon," he said. "A sandstorm might be coming in from the west."

"We'll stop in a few hours," Stone said.

"Are you ready?" Mehabiah asked.

"Yes," Stone smiled.

"The first task is supposed to be the worst," Mehabiah said.

"I know."

"You'll be alright?" Mehabiah asked with a grin.

"We'll be alright," Stone replied.

"If Stone dies, you'll take over," John said.

"He won't die," Joshua replied.

"And if he does?"

"Does he know about this?" Joshua asked.

"He doesn't want to know," John replied. "He told me that it doesn't make sense for him to know. 'Talk to Joshua about the details.' Those were his words."

"And when he returns?" Joshua asked.

"Then we have nothing to worry about," John replied.

"And Mehabiah?"

"If they kill Stone on the journey," John replied, "…they'll most certainly kill Mehabiah."

"And we really need this."

"Yes," said John. "I want only a few of you in on it—just a group of Gatherers. No one else will know. Not even Stone's caravan. If the Elders kill Stone, they'll be unaware of our plans."

Joshua pondered over John's suggestion for a few moments.

"So," John said. "What do you think?"

"Sit down," Joshua replied.

"But he doesn't believe in God," Paris said.

"He does," Stone replied.

"Ask anybody."

"I don't need to," Stone said.

"You can't have a godless man around you."

"Fall back into rank, Paris," Stone commanded.

Paris was angry. He turned his camel swiftly around and rode toward Ahab and the caravan.

"They're in love," Paris said sarcastically.

"They grew up together," Ahab said.

"He doesn't listen."

"He's stubborn…"

"And proud," Paris said.

"It'll take time," Ahab said. "But he'll understand."

The sun was sinking behind the Kalabaash Mountains. Stone stopped his camel.

"We'll camp here for the evening!" Stone shouted.

The men dismounted their camels. Mehabiah prepared everyone for the encampment. Paris and Ahab were placed a hundred yards from Stone's tent. Mehabiah placed his own tent next to Stone's, and Arjuna was instructed to guard Stone during the night.

"Sleep with your sword," Mehabiah said.

"I will," replied Stone.

"And rest well," Mehabiah said. "Tomorrow's an important day."

Stone smiled and closed his eyes as Mehabiah stepped out into the dark night. The murmurs in the camp eventually died down as everyone gradually fell asleep. Mehabiah was anxious. Everyone was counting on him to guard Stone while the tasks were being completed. "Don't be careless," John had said.

He walked back toward Stone's tent. He pulled out a copy of *El-Theikos* and started reciting the scriptures. He prayed for Stone's well-being.

Mehabiah cherished his relationship with God. He had always been a pious man. And now, as he read the scriptures, he felt the smooth vibrations of the divine power stroking his heart and relaxing his tension. "But I must not relax," he told himself. "Not until I return to Shur." He looked up at the sky.

"God," he whispered. "Be with my brother."

The moonlight glittered off the river and the bridge loomed above the men like a gravestone. Hector, one of the older Gatherers, squinted his eyes and stared into the darkness. He could see Joshua walking toward him. The Gatherers rose to their feet. They stepped forward.

"What's this about, Joshua?" asked Hector.

"In silence." Joshua said.

"Silence," the rest of the Gatherers replied back.

"John?" Hector asked.

"Yes," Joshua replied.

"We're needed?" Hector asked.

"More than we have been for a while," Joshua said.
"What for?"
"If Stone dies," Joshua said. "During the tasks or otherwise."
"He's not going to."
"I know," Joshua replied.
"We're around a thousand in all."
"And we're all silent?"
"All of us except for you."
"Let's keep it that way."

"Make sure you see her," Stone had asked Joshua. "I will," Joshua had replied. "I don't want to, but I will." "You need to forget her," Joshua had said. "How can I?" "It's not good for you." "I love her." "Do you?" "Catonell, Catonell." "She doesn't know what she wants." "I know." "Why do you love her?" "I don't know." "Forget her." "She made me feel safe."

"Is he safe?"

"I think he is," Mehabiah replied.

"Let's check on him," Arjuna said.

Stone's thoughts were interrupted by the sounds of men approaching his tent. He grasped his sword. The sounds became more audible. He relaxed his grip. The voices belonged to Mehabiah and Arjuna. Mehabiah lifted the tents flap and looked inside. Stone kept his eyes closed.

"He's asleep," Mehabiah whispered to Arjuna.

"We'll stay out here," Arjuna replied.

Stone opened his eyes and looked around his tent. He took a deep breath and yawned. He was proud of Mehabiah. In private, Stone would speak of him constantly. "My brother's so handsome," he would say. "I'm ugly compared to him." And the women would laugh. "You're not bad yourself," they would say. "You're not bad at all." And he would give them a sad smile. He didn't care much for the women he had been with the last few years.

Joshua had warned him to stay away from women. They were a distraction. But he couldn't. He moved from one woman to another, in a futile attempt to erase any memory of Catonell. He hated loving her. She had found her way deep into the core of his being, and she wouldn't leave. He fell asleep thinking of her. He dreamed of her also.

Joshua walked home alone. He went to his mother's room and kissed her on the forehead. He then walked into his study and pulled out a few books from the shelf. He chose <u>Romeo and Juliet</u>, and immersed himself in the tragedy of the Capulets and the Montagues. He thought of Stone and Catonell when he read the tragedy. He felt sorry for Stone. He couldn't understand Stone's uncompromising love for her.

"A plague o' both your houses! Zounds, a dog, a rat, a mouse, a cat to scratch a man to death!" Mercutio was dying. "Poor Mercutio," Joshua whispered, as he continued reading under the bright moonlight, which streamed into the room through a large window behind him.

CHAPTER 7

Tasks

Love not, that which you cannot have.

—*El-Theikos*, Chapter 45: Proverbs, verses 1–3

They wrapped a white cloth around the man and stabbed him nine times. He fell to the ground.

"What's his crime?"

"Rape," Joshua replied.

Joshua didn't like watching executions. He turned away from the dying man and looked up at the bright sun. He wondered if Stone's caravan had reached the mountains.

"Catonell?" David asked.

"What?" Joshua replied.

"You're seeing Catonell today?"

"Yes."

"Do you want to do that next?"

"I'm not sure." Joshua replied.

"Does Stone know?" David asked.

"He asked me to."

"No, I mean about her wedding."

"Oh, yes," Joshua replied.

"What does he think?"

"He's all right."

"Good."

"David?

"Yes."

"I'd like to see her alone," Joshua said. "You can take the rest of the day off."

"Are you sure?"

"Yes," Joshua replied. "Thank you."

David shook Joshua's hand and walked away. Joshua looked back at the dead man lying on the ground. He couldn't stand the smell of blood.

He walked toward the corpse and looked into its lifeless eyes. He had once seen himself die in a dream. He had felt no pain. He did not fear death. He was an atheist—no superstitions, no ghosts, no spirits. He took a deep breath and stepped away from the corpse. "In a blink of an eye," he thought.

"Is this good, Joshua?" a man asked, pointing to a brown sack.

"Yes."

The man lifted the corpse, placed it in the sack, and carried it away.

Joshua made sure the corpse was buried properly. Then he started walking in the direction of Catonell's house. He arrived at her front door by mid-after-noon.

"Come on in, Joshua," Catherine said.

"Thank you," Joshua replied. "Is your sister at home?"

"Yes," Catherine replied. "She's not well. She has a fever."

"Can I see her?"

"Is it about Stone?"

"He sent me."

"She's in her room," Catherine said. "Don't bother her too much."

Joshua didn't answer her. He walked toward Catonell's room. The room was dark. She lay on her bed with a wet cloth on her head.

"Hello," Joshua said.

"Joshua?"

"Yes," he said. "It's me."

"Is Stone…"

"No," Joshua said. "He's still in the mountains."

"I'm not well."

"I know," Joshua said. "Your sister told me. Can I do anything for you?"

"No, I'll be fine."

Joshua sat down next to her bed.

"How's Stone?"

"He's fine," Joshua said.

"When was the last time I saw you?" she asked.

"About a year."

"That's sad."

Joshua didn't reply.

"You're a good friend to him."

"I try."

"Does he still not understand?" Catonell asked.

"No," Joshua replied. "Even I don't."

"I really care about him."

"I thought you did," Joshua said.

"You don't believe me."

"I'm not sure."

"I do care about him," Catonell repeated herself.

"Then why did you leave him?" Joshua asked.

"I can't marry him."

"Do you still love him?" Joshua asked.

"Will you tell him if I tell you?"

"I don't know."

"It'll hurt him if you do."

"Do you?"

"I'm not telling you."

"You don't need to," Joshua said.

They had been friends for many years. Joshua knew her well.

"I've been through a lot."

"Everyone has," Joshua said.

"I can't let things change now," Catonell said. "You reach a certain age and you just can't."

"We've talked about this before," Joshua said. "If you still love him, you should tell him."

"And what will that accomplish," she said.

"He wanted to marry you."

"I can't marry him."

"Why?"

"Do you expect me to wait here, in this house, for you to come in some day and tell me that he's dead? Both you and Mehabiah?"

"Is that really the reason?"

"Yes."

"I don't believe you."

"Well, you should."

Catonell slowly rolled over to her side so that she could face Joshua.

"Why did you stop coming?" she asked.

"Because you hurt my friend."

"Am I not your friend?"

"You lured him in."

"I did not," Catonell said. "You didn't answer my question."

"Which one?"

"Why did you stop coming?" Catonell said. "We've been friends since we were six."

"I don't know why."

"You used to come by all the time," Catonell said. "My mother asked about you before she died. 'He's a sweet boy,' she said. She actually asked me what I had done to make you go away. I almost laughed when she said that."

"You didn't do anything."

"Do you hate me?"

"No," Joshua said. "I don't hate anybody."

"Whenever your parents were looking for you they would come here," Catonell said. "Jesus would come knocking on the door."

Joshua remained silent.

"I've got the most awful headache."

"Do you want me to change the cloth?" Joshua asked.

"Please," Catonell replied.

Joshua wet a fresh towel with cold water and placed it on her head.

"You should sleep," he said.

"I want to talk."

"I'll come back."

"Next year?" she smiled.

"Tomorrow," he said.

"Stay," she said. "Please."

Joshua nodded his head and sat down again.

"I was thinking of you the other day," Catonell said. "It was Jesus's birthday."

"It was."

"You loved him very much."

Joshua didn't reply.

"I remember the day he died," Catonell said. "You walked up to his room and ran out of your house with his diary. You read every single page of it, again and again. You cried. I remember."

Catonell and Joshua were silent. He tried not to think about the day his brother died. He looked at Catonell. She had been an important part of his life. He looked at her as she struggled to keep her eyes open. The fever had drained her.

"Get your rest," Joshua said.

"Will you come back tomorrow?"

"I will," he replied.

Joshua walked toward the door. He stopped.

"I'm sorry I wasn't there when your mother died," he said.

"I forgive you," she said with a smile.

"You were there for me," he said. "I should have come by."

"She really loved you," she said.

"I know," he said.

"Come by soon," she said.

"I will," he said with a sad smile. He wanted to walk back to her and touch her before he left. But he didn't. Instead he walked out of her house with a heavy heart.

❧   ❧   ❧

He was surrounded by complete darkness. He walked slowly. He strained his eyes but could see nothing. His heart beat furiously against his chest. He measured his steps. "Two hundred." He should have reached the lair by now. He crouched. He waited. He clenched his teeth and strained his ears for a sound, any sound. A loud roar disturbed the silence. He turned around. He could hear two sets of heartbeats. He drew his sword.

He reached into his pocket and pulled out a rock. He flung it against the cave wall. He heard the beast pounce at the rock. He moved toward the heinous growl that had devoured the ghastly silence. He swung his sword into the darkness repeatedly. The sword made contact. He heard the growl turn into a devilish moan. Then he felt a great force strike him as he fell to the ground. The beast lay on his chest. He could not breathe. He held the beast with his left hand, pulled out his dagger, and tore into its neck. The animal gnarled at his throat and sunk its fangs into his shoulder. He felt his flesh tear. Warm blood flowed down his arm.

He held the beast by its mane and with a gigantic effort flung it across the cave. He heard it fall and rise again. He pulled out a second dagger and waited for it to pounce.

"One last pounce," he thought to himself. He knew it was dying. "Come on!" he screamed. He heard the beast come closer. It charged at him. He felt its warm, stale breath a few inches away. He felt its fangs in his throat and its giant paws on his shoulders. He pushed his dagger into the beast and dragged it down into its chest. It growled. He pulled away and left a piece of his flesh in the animal's mouth. Then he pulled a hatchet from his belt and hammered the animal to death.

He stood alone in the darkness for a while. A sharp pain had taken over the left side of his body. He lifted the beast and carried it over his shoulders. He walked toward the mouth of the cave. He enjoyed combat. He was smiling. He felt good about his victory. He could see the sunlight stream into the cave. He walked faster. He reached the mouth of the cave and stood motionless.

Five hundred men had their eyes on him. They let out a great cheer. The cheers echoed off of the cliffs of Mount Nur. Stone threw the beast to the ground, and lifted his arms. Their champion had returned.

CHAPTER 8

❀

Assassination

Formidable is the enemy that lies concealed behind righteousness.

—*El-Theikos*, Chapter 30: The Wars, verse 17

After keeping watch late one night, Hector came to Joshua with the news. A statue of Jenut had been desecrated. On it someone had painted the word "Zarasthura[1]." Such instances were becoming more frequent. Usually the graffiti was accompanied by anti-religious sentiments, closely matching quotations from some of the books in Joshua's library.

He accompanied Hector to the statue and felt sad that his teachings were being translated into obscene works of crime.

"It's so unnecessary," Joshua said.

"They don't understand," Hector replied.

"I'll speak of this at the next teaching," Joshua said.

"Do you think it'll matter?"

"It should."

"Maybe they don't understand," Hector said again.

"They must," Joshua said. "We'll go over the works of civil disobedience. They'll understand."

---

1.   A reference to Neitzsche

"You're giving them a voice," Hector said.

"They should have one."

"Are they ready for one?" asked Hector.

"They'll learn," Joshua said.

The two men climbed the statue and started cleaning off the graffiti. It was early in the morning, and Joshua wondered if Stone was still awake.

❦   ❦   ❦

They had come silently. Mehabiah spotted them and nudged Arjuna from his sleep. The two men walked toward Stone's tent, drew their swords, and confronted the assassins. The assassins tried to fight Arjuna and Mehabiah off but they couldn't. Swiftly and forcefully, Arjuna and Mehabiah disarmed the six men.

They kept the assassins alive and then sounded the signal. The entire camp quickly arose and congregated around Stone's tent, where Arjuna and Mehabiah had the assassins on their knees.

With everyone paying close attention, Mehabiah spoke.

"Assassins!" he shouted at the crowd pointing at the bleeding men. "If anyone else is with them, come forth now, and your punishment will be less severe."

No one moved. Arjuna walked toward one of the assassins and pointed his sword below his abdomen.

"Speak now," Mehabiah said.

The man did not speak. His silence was greeted with extreme pain as he squealed in agony. Arjuna removed his bloodied sword and placed it close to the man's hand.

"Speak now," Mehabiah said again.

The man did not speak. Arjuna slowly removed his index finger from his hand. The assassin was now in excruciating pain and begged for mercy.

"Sufiyan was with us," he said softly, trying desperately to get words out between the panting that accompanied his agony. "And so was Duryodhana, Qasim, and Saul."

A few men from the crowd tried to make an escape but were held down by those loyal to Stone. These men were brought forward.

The torturing continued until eleven men were revealed. But Mehabiah did not get the name he was looking for. He wanted one of them to shout "Paris! Paris was with us."

But no one did. Mehabiah was almost certain that Paris had masterminded the assassination attempt. He also knew that if Paris had arranged the debacle, he was intelligent enough not to get directly involved. Paris had probably hired the assassins through anonymous correspondence, promising the men great riches if they succeeded in the unholy venture.

Throughout the afternoon, the assassins revealed the names of many conspirators, but couldn't give him the one name he wanted. And so Mehabiah would never know if Paris had planned the assassination.

When the twenty assassins were assembled, Mehabiah and Arjuna asked a group of foot soldiers to come forward. They drew their swords and executed the men. The heads were saved for the next town hall meeting. Mehabiah wanted to make an example of the traitors and wanted everyone to recognize Stone's infallibility.

All along, during the brutal interrogation, Stone was preparing himself for the next task, meditating a few miles north of the camp, closer to the mountains, far away from the evil machinations of political corruption.

CHAPTER 9

❁

Mother

But O' deaths untimely frost, nipped my flower so early.[1]

—*El-Theikos*, Chapter 14: Lamentations, verse 10

An atheist once told her that God had died in the morning, before Helios had graced the purple skies. Man woke up and he didn't know; so he continued living, because the sun continued to rise and set as if God were still alive. Meena didn't believe him. She didn't think man could survive the loss of God. But he told her that man could get used to anything.

It had been four years since her son, Jesus's death, and she was afraid that she was getting used to a world without him. The scent had finally left the clothes that hung in his room, and he was gradually becoming more of a memory.

Many times she would try to rationalize his death. She would tell herself that it really didn't matter if a man died at twenty or at seventy. Thousands of people would go on living, and thousands of people would go on dying, conveniently buried in a cemetery with other forgotten souls—a cold stone marking the expanse of a lifetime.

---

1. Originially a line from an ancient poem that found its way into the Holy Scriptures.

But she also knew that the only time it mattered if a man died at twenty or seventy was if that man was her son. She hadn't been ready for his death, and like any sane mother she tried to keep him alive for as long as she could by speaking about him constantly.

But then, one day while shopping in the bazaar, she remembered the stories of her mother Ayesha. Ayesha would revive memories of Meena's grandfather, Anim. "Don't forget him," she would say softly, hiding the soft sparkle in her eye.

Surrounded by the smell of fresh fruit and within the hollering of market vendors, Meena realized that she hadn't thought about her grandfather for years. And whenever she had, it was only in passing—a connection between generations, marked by a memory of a face created in her mind. She felt sad because she realized that Jesus was truly dead, and no matter how hard she tried nothing would change the cold, hard fact that memories cannot be fleshed out into living beings. Dead people become, and always remain, apparitions—reflections of a lost body, gradually growing dimmer and moving deeper into the looking glass of the afterlife, until they cannot be seen anymore.

Yet, Joshua's uncanny ability to keep his brother alive amazed her. He kept Jesus in the recesses of his mind, and he would unconsciously resuscitate him through his thoughts, discussions, and actions. Gradually, it became obvious that he was using his brother's teachings in his daily affairs. He would smile when people told him that he reminded them of Jesus. Joshua felt that if he reminded them of his brother, then in some strange way Jesus was still alive.

It upset Joshua that his mother had stopped talking about his brother. He thought that she was trying to forget him. But she wasn't. She would do anything in the world to keep his face fresh in her mind, to keep the smell of his hair tucked safely away, thinking of it like she thought about the river: a memory made vivid with sensation. She would try everything. She would sometimes sleep with his clothes at night. She would think of the day he was born and she would remember the unbearable pain that had marked his birth. She would think of the times she had been angry with him and the times she had held him when he cried. But then that one painful thought would enter her head. She was being too deliberate with her memories. She felt like she was breathing for him and speaking for him, and she realized that she couldn't do either, because, after all, the truth didn't change. Her son was dead. She knew that many of their memories together would gradually fade away, and naturally she would keep some of them. Then one day she would die and those memories would disappear into nothingness as well.

In her saddest moments she would visit the temples and light candles and incense. The priests would leave her alone, and she would pray. Surrounded by pillars of faith and religious scriptures, she would pray for one thing only: she wanted Joshua to outlive her. She knew that she couldn't bear seeing another son perish before her eyes and eventually within her memories.

CHAPTER 10

❀

The Birds

And he slew the Stymphalians and chased them across the mountains into the lands beyond.

—*El-Theikos*, Chapter 111: The Journeys, verse 34

Paris sat in his tent and prayed. A small lantern lay before him, beside his shrine of Jenut. Behind the small statue of the prophet stood three stems of incense. Paris liked the smell of burning incense.

He closed his eyes. Every day at sunset for the last fifty years Paris spoke with God. And God would speak to him as well, guiding his actions and his conscience, providing him with a sense of peace and direction.

Surrounded by God, he prayed for his friends and for the future of Shur and for the souls of the Shurites. He would pray for Stone and ask God to guide Stone's soul. He would also pray for Joshua, with the hope that the boy would finally find God and disregard the temptations of Lucifer. In Paris's eyes, Joshua was a sad example of genius gone wrong—wasted over nihilism instead of God. He knew that Joshua intentionally blinded himself and that he willfully resisted God's intervention. "How can he be so intelligent and not recognize God?" he thought to himself. "Lord, save his soul in this life, and after," Paris whispered. He then blew out the incense, stood up, and walked out of his tent.

The smell of blood from Mehabiah's violent interrogation was still in the air. Paris looked around at the other tents, each with a torch standing next to it. The tents stretched out before him for a mile. In the distance he could see the sun barely grazing the peaks of Kalabaash as it bid adieu to the world for one more night.

"Councilman Paris," Arjuna said as he walked by.

"Arjuna," Paris said.

Arjuna stopped and turned around.

"Yes?"

"Is Stone back yet?" Paris asked.

"No," Arjuna said. "I think he'll probably stay in the mountains and complete the tasks."

"But he should rest."

"The second task is more a matter of his mind than physical strength," Arjuna said. "He's probably done with the second task by now."

"He still needs his rest," Paris said.

"Mehabiah followed him after the interrogation this morning," Arjuna said. "He'll make sure that Stone is safe. If he's tired I'm sure Mehabiah will bring him back for the night. But then the journey's long and they're going to the other side. I think they'll camp in the mountains."

"Arjuna," Paris said softly.

Arjuna waited for Paris to speak.

"Why wasn't I told that Stone wasn't in the camp last night?" Paris asked.

Arjuna smiled.

"No one was told, Councilman Paris," Arjuna said. "That's the way Mehabiah wanted it."

"Is it a matter of trust?"

"No," Arjuna interrupted. "It's a matter of Mehabiah's will. Stone's his brother. I would've done the same thing."

"It's probably best for Stone," Paris said. "I understand."

"If it makes you feel better, Councilman Paris," Arjuna said. "I didn't know either."

"Thank you Arjuna," Paris said.

"Now get some rest," Arjuna replied. "If all goes well with Stone we'll probably return to the city tomorrow."

❦   ❦   ❦

Thousands of years ago on this land through God's wrath had come hail and fire mixed with blood, hurled down upon the earth. Huge mountains, all ablaze, had been thrown into the sea, and a great star blazing like a torch had fallen from the skies on the rivers and on the springs of water. A third of the sun was also struck, and a third of the moon and a third of the stars, and a third of the day was without light. And God screamed into the cosmos, "Woe to the inhabitants of Earth! Woe!" And then He unleashed smoke and fire from a great Abyss that rose into the heavens and devoured the clouds and turned the blue skies gray. And from these gray skies and black dust, rose the Stymphalians. Flesh-eating beasts, relishing the taste of blood—a fatal pest to all of mankind and the last of the caravans.

The Stymphalian birds had brazen beaks and claws and wings, and they would devour humans quickly, leaving behind clean-boned carcasses. After man's first sin and God's ensuing punishment, the old world had given way to seemingly endless migrations that often fell prey to the Stymphalians. According to folklore, during the plight for fertile land, the Asian tribes had been lost in the Pacific desert. Many suspected the Stymphalians as the villains of this mass genocide. According to John and the old books, only Daud's tribes had successfully driven the birds away. Yet, a few had followed his caravan through Kalabaash. One night, however, armed with a bow and arrow, Daud chased the birds out of Urdin, across the mountains into the forgotten lands. Ever since Daud confronted them, the Stymphalians had taken residence on the other side of Kalabaash, where the mountains were still ragged from God's rage.

Stone remembered these stories well as he carefully descended the sharp, black cliffs. He had traveled five days through the Kalabaash range, and now he could feel and eventually see the treacherous mountains on the other side. He had never before seen these lands with gray sand and black rock. The warm wind blew in his face and howled against the rocky peaks. John had told him that the sun god would never again look down on this forgotten land, neither when he ascended the starry heaven nor when he returned to earth. Dire, eternal night would always cover this domain.

As he scaled the steep cliffs, Stone was glad that he had already completed two tasks. Slaying the lion had been relatively simple. But, he had almost lost his life during the second task, which involved practicing an ancient meditation ceremony, referred to in *El-Theikos* as the Leap of Faith. He had all but stopped the beating of his heart. Every priest for the last one thousand years had died while in the trance, but Stone had found a way a back.

"Focus," he told himself. He didn't want any recollection of the Leap of Faith.

He held on to the cliffs with his bare hands and swung himself from one protruding rock to another, until he carefully made his way to a landing. He looked up at the stars and followed the directions given to him by the clergy. After a little while he found himself standing in front of a cave. "The bird's nest will be within the Cave of Josiah," Paris had said. "Tread carefully."

Stone slowly removed his bow from his shoulder and strapped six arrows on his hip. He took a deep breath and walked into the cave.

CHAPTER 11

❁

King

And the Lord made him infallible, and gave him the power of the heavens so that he could lead his people and make them believe in Nanak. "Dream no more!"

—*El-Theikos*, Chapter 15: Restoration, verses 15–16

The sun slithered down the Kalabaash Mountains. Steam rose behind Stone as the rain from the night before evaporated into the air. A cool breeze swept the dust off of his brown face. He walked slowly and deliberately toward Arjuna, Mehabiah and Jonathan. As he approached them, the men felt the sense of power that naturally emanated from him like a cloud covering his being and penetrating those in touch with him. In his thin black robes, the lion's hide flung across his shoulders, the sun glowing behind him, he looked more God than man.

They bowed down. They kissed his hand. They slowly stood up, each one of them visualizing a past memory in which Stone had rescued them from imminent death. A flash of a sword, the thunder of his horse quickly whisking by, removing the terror grappling their mortality. Water, slipping, sinking, a hand—his hand. Religious infidelity, Elder's wrath, his compassion.

They had seen him become a man when he was only six. They had seen him carry them on his shoulders when he was ten. School fights with bullies usually ended with him challenging the larger, stronger boys and defeating them with his wiry strength and unquenchable will to conquer everything. His steely, cold eyes would conceal the storm brewing within, over which his control was absolute and his desire to unleash conditional. And then he would fight, intelligently, until he would win.

Once, during a particularly brutal skirmish four months before his thirteenth birthday, the boys noticed that he was bleeding profusely. They tried to intervene, but he pushed them back, giving them a quick glance that in itself could knock over any man. Even the bully wanted to stop, but Stone refused, instead mocking the bully to continue fighting. He shrugged his shoulders, wiped the blood from his forehead with his arm, looked at his friends, and walked toward his prey.

The sun was high in the sky beating down on the two boys as they struggled furiously in the sand for hours, each exhausted, eventually harnessing strengths from the pits of their souls—strengths that keep men alive long after animals wither. The fight continued until the bully lay dazed, bewildered, and almost unconscious. He had been outwilled, outsmarted by Stone, the son of Proteus, from the line of Daud. The chosen one knew that he couldn't fail in front of the people of Shur. He encapsulated their dreams, their hopes, their desires—everything that they could never be, he had to become. As long as they could look at him and see their failures defeated by his being and their fears conquered by his strength, their lives would be bearable.

Mehabiah, Arjuna, and Jonathan allowed Stone to walk by. They followed him to the camp. The Elders were waiting. Their wrinkled skin and wrinkled hearts could not bear the grip he had over the Shurites.

"He has nine lives," said Ahab.

"He's down to five," replied Paris.

Paris pulled out the blue brace of Jenut from a golden bag. A large crowd had gathered around the men. Paris carefully began placing the brace across Stone's shoulders. Then he opened a long, thin, black box and removed the sword of Jenut from it, placing it in Stone's hand. Both Paris and Ahab slowly knelt down. They had been surprised at the speed with which Stone had completed the three tasks. The beast in the cave, the Leap of Faith, and the Stymphalian birds had all been conquered.

"The tasks are complete," said Ahab.

"Our King is chosen," said Paris. "We're one step closer to Nanak."

Every man from the caravan bowed down. Arjuna stood behind Stone, and for the first time in his life he felt the presence of God.

CHAPTER 12

❀

The Return

On that day, brothers will rise against one another, fathers will bury their sons, and friends will turn their backs...

—*El-Theikos*, Chapter 30: Prophesies, verses 2–3

John had taught him everything. Sitting on the edge of the river on a sun-drenched afternoon, he recalled the day John had challenged his reality. He had shifted Joshua's paradigms by challenging him to observe beyond the obvious. Through years of listening and learning, Joshua's reality eventually took a turn for the absurd. Every object around him always seemed alive, and every perspective seemed alien and fresh. Every time he saw the sunlight reflect off the water he noticed strange and exquisite new patterns. It was as if John had helped him discover a fascinating new orb under the boring, monotonous world superimposed onto reality by the inadequate imaginations of mediocre people.

At about sixteen, his eyes and all his sensations had encountered a new world. It was as if he had awoken from a long dream. And now, at thirty, Joshua truly appreciated John's teachings. He liked being aware of his reality and the numerous perspectives through which one filters information into the mind. He knew that he could never experience every single perspective; yet he was adamant to experience as many as he could.

The sun was unusually bright for the late afternoon. He noticed his shadow and the way in which it disappeared over the water.

"Joshua!"

Joshua turned around. He didn't like having his thoughts interrupted. Hector ran toward him.

"What is it?" Joshua asked.

"The caravan's returning."

"Any news?" Joshua asked.

"The scout says he saw Mehabiah."

"How far from the city?"

"They're four hours away," Hector said.

Joshua and Hector started walking toward the army barracks in Ancient Shur.

"Are the Gatherers ready?" Joshua asked.

"Yes," Hector replied.

"Don't forget," Joshua said. "The caravan doesn't enter the city until we're sure that Mehabiah and Stone are alive."

"Yes."

"Is my horse ready?" Joshua asked.

"And if Stone is not alive?"

"I'll give the signal."

The two men walked to the barracks and in the next few hours the largest regiment of the army was assembled. As a core commander of the army, Joshua had mastered the art of mobilization. Once assembled, Joshua led the army to the outskirts of the city. A small group of Gatherers decked in black robes with their faces covered followed closely behind, keeping their distance from the infantry. Their swords gleamed in the bloom of the bright afternoon.

The camels slowly moved to the edge of the city limits. Joshua rode a black horse at the front of the Shurite army. In the distance he could see Stone's caravan returning, like a trail of ants making their way to Shur. He noticed that the caravan had dispatched a messenger on a white horse. The messenger made his way quickly toward the Shurite army. He carried a white flag.

"Why a white flag?" Joshua asked.

"I'm not sure," Hector replied.

"We're not at war."

Joshua felt a strange sensation at the base of his spine. Maybe John was right. He pondered over the possibility of Stone being dead.

"Do you think…?" Hector asked.

"Let's wait and find out."

Joshua turned his head and looked at the legion of Gatherers behind him. They maintained a noticeable distance from the rest of the army. They were waiting for Joshua's signal.

"Here he comes," Hector said.

"I'll go forward," Joshua said.

Joshua rode his horse toward the messenger. Hector galloped slowly behind him. He pulled out his bow and arrow.

Joshua was now ten feet away from the man on the white horse. It was Arjuna.

"Why the army?" Arjuna asked.

"I'll tell you later on," Joshua said. "What's the message?"

"Stone and Mehabiah are alive," Arjuna said.

"We want you to send them out."

"Why?"

"I want to see them."

"What's going on, Joshua?" Arjuna asked.

"We want to make sure," Joshua replied.

"Is my word not good enough?" Arjuna asked firmly.

"This is more important than your word and my trust," Joshua said. "Please go back and tell them that the caravan does not enter Shur until I'm sure that Stone and Mehabiah are alive."

"You have to send someone in," Arjuna said.

"What do you mean?" Joshua asked.

"Stone's orders," Arjuna said. "If you want to see him, send a messenger in."

Joshua looked at Hector, and then back at the caravan.

"Follow him to the caravan," he said. "I'll wait through sunset and then I'm sending in the Gatherers."

Hector nodded his head. He trotted his horse slowly toward Arjuna. The two men rode together toward the caravan.

❧   ❧   ❧

The afternoon sun glared down on Stone's face. White robes protected his skin from the harsh desert air. He stood on a rock and squinted his eyes. Two thousand yards of sand separated him from the magnificence of the Shur army. The gleaming swords, one next to another, in perfect lines and in immaculate order, were all representations of Joshua's military guile. Stone looked at the army with pride and bewilderment. He had been away for over six months. He should have spoken with Joshua and John about the return. He didn't like being in the dark.

The presence of the army bothered him. He mulled over every possible scenario. He couldn't imagine Joshua betraying him. But he couldn't eliminate that possibility either.

He stepped down from the rock and walked back toward the caravan. Mehabiah stood waiting for him.

"Get me every man I trust," Stone said. "Paris also."

Mehabiah nodded his head and gathered Stone's regular advisors. The men rendezvoused in Stone's tent.

"What do you think?" Stone asked.

"The army?" Mehabiah said. "Why an entire regiment?"

"It's beginning," Paris said.

"Nothing is *beginning*, Paris," Stone said sarcastically.

"I saw the Gatherers in their black with their faces covered," Paris said. "It's a sign of death."

"Why would Joshua kill me?"

"A king has been anointed," Paris replied. "The atheist shakes in his boots, because God is returning to Shur. Is that not reason enough?"

"Joshua's not an atheist," Stone said.

"We need to be cautious," Arjuna said.

"An entire regiment?" Mehabiah said again. "It's probably to make sure we're fine. I don't think Joshua would allow the caravan back into the city if something had happened to you or any of us."

"We should still keep you at the back of the caravan," Arjuna said, addressing Stone.

"I agree," Mehabiah said. "No harm in being cautious."

"I trust Joshua," Stone said.

"Of course," Arjuna said. "We all do."

Paris was being beckoned outside the tent. He quickly walked out.

"Mehabiah's right," Stone said. "It's probably John's plan. He had briefly mentioned that Joshua would prepare for the worst possible scenarios."

"We should've known about this," Arjuna said.

"There was no need for us to know," Stone replied. "Let's send a messenger,"

"I'll go," Mehabiah said.

"Not you," Stone said.

"Let me go," Arjuna said.

"Very well," Stone said. "Tell Joshua that I'm alive and ready to enter the city."

"He'll want to see you," Mehabiah said.

Stone looked around at the men in the tent.

"Have them send someone, if they want to see me," Stone said. "I think that should be acceptable."

"I trust Joshua," Mehabiah said.

"We all do," Stone said.

"We should be cautious," Arjuna said.

※   ※   ※

"Where is he?" asked Hector.

"Give me your weapons," Arjuna said.

"If I don't return, he'll send the Gatherers."

"And..."

"You don't fear Gatherers, Arjuna?"

"I never have."

"They're everywhere."

"I know."

"But you don't," said Hector with a smile.

"Are you a Gatherer?" asked Arjuna.

"I couldn't tell you."

"Why only the leader?"

"What about it?"

"Why can the leader only share his identity?"

"Because he sits on the Council," Hector answered. "It's important for the Gatherers to be close to city affairs."

"Joshua the Gatherer."

"John told me stories when I was young."

"I heard them," Arjuna said. "Jenut's choice to maintain justice in the city."

"He never trusted the Elders," Hector said.

"Who does?" Arjuna said.

"Is Stone alive?" Hector asked.

"Yes," Arjuna replied. "Why the army?"

"John's plan."

"You'd destroy the caravan if Stone was dead?"

"Yes."

Arjuna nodded his head indicating approval.

"I'm glad you agree."

"If Stone was dead, I'd be dead, too," Arjuna said.

"You're a good man."

"I'm faithful."

"We all are," replied Hector as the two men walked into Stone's tent.

CHAPTER 13

❀

Confessions

O' Lord hear my prayer, listen to my cry for mercy.

—*El-Theikos*, Chapter 14: Lamentations, verse 1

The sound of the temple door opening interrupted Mehabiah's confession. He could hear footsteps outside the confessional chambers.

"Mehabiah?" a woman's voice called out firmly.

It was his mother.

Mehabiah stood up and walked out of the confessional chambers. His mother stood before him. She was a beautiful woman. Tall and strong, her dark bright eyes reflected her strong will.

"Come home with me," she said firmly.

"I'm confessing."

"Come home!" she said again.

Mehabiah walked toward her. She took him to a quiet corner of the temple and looked at him sternly. He said nothing.

"You're a leader of these people."

Mehabiah nodded his head.

"And you're going to confess your deepest secrets to a priest?" she said.

"He's a man of God."

"Do you think Paris is a man of God?" she asked.

"Paris is corrupt."

"What makes this priest so special?"

"He can't see me," Mehabiah said. "The chambers are separated."

"They know it's you, Mehabiah," she said. "They've heard your voice a thousand times."

"I needed to talk," he said.

"You're tired," she said. "The journey has made your judgment weak."

"I haven't slept for eight days."

His mother sighed. "I know."

"My body hurts, Mother," he said.

His mother held his face in her hands.

"Let's sit down," she said.

She sat down in one of the aisles. Mehabiah sat down beside her. The tasks and the assassination attempt in the desert had drained him of his energy.

"It's difficult being a leader," she said.

"Father did it well."

"He had bad days," she said. "But he knew not to show it. He always walked like a king, and he talked like a king, and he never showed anyone when he was tired, angry or scared. A strong leader cannot afford to, especially at the beginning. And your father was fortunate. He had Joshua's father Acrisius to support him. Jesus was a lot like Acrisius. He could converse about anything with anybody. Acrisius loved reading, and your father loved him for showing him new worlds. But the Elders hated him, just like they hate Joshua. And we'll all…"

Mehabiah's mother stopped talking. A priest stood before her. Mehabiah sat up.

"Hello, sister Roxanna," the priest said.

"Hello, Father," Roxanna said.

"I was just speaking with your son."

"I know," Roxanna replied. "He was testing you."

Mehabiah looked at his mother and smiled.

"Testing me?"

"To see if you'd come out of the chamber," she said.

"I don't understand."

"You're not supposed to know the identity of the confessioners, Father," she said.

"Yes."

"You failed your test."

"But I couldn't…"

"You should sit in there until dismissed," she pointed to the confessional chambers.

"I'm terribly…"

"What did he tell you, Father?"

"I can't tell you, sister Roxanna."

"I'm his mother, you can tell me."

The priest looked at Mehabiah. He nodded his head.

"He told me that he was angry with a friend."

"He did?"

"Yes."

"And who else will hear of this confession?"

"Nobody,"

"Everybody…" Roxanna replied.

"No, sister."

"Mehabiah?"

"Yes, mother," Mehabiah replied.

"I think you should report this priest to the Council," she said. "He's violating temple rules."

"But, sister…," the priest said.

"Tell the Council about your test and the fake confession, and tell them that he failed."

"No," the priest said.

"Why not?"

"I won't be careless again," the priest said.

"What do you think, Mehabiah?" Roxanna said.

"Whatever pleases you, Mother."

"Fine then," she said. "We'll ignore your transgression."

"Yes," the priest said.

"What was that, Father?" his mother said.

"Thank you," the priest replied.

"And if I hear you talking about it," she said. "Because if you do, I will…"

"You won't hear me repeat anything," said the priest. "I promise you won't."

"Good," Roxanna said.

The priest smiled sheepishly.

"You can leave now," Roxanna said as the priest quickly turned around and walked back into the confessional chambers.

CHAPTER 14

❀

John's Diary

Histories: repetitious poems. Reflections of past crimes, and warnings of future follies.

—*El-Theikos*, Chapter 24: Histories, verse 59

15th day of Daud, 976 YK

In a moonless sky, on a cloudless night, a son is born to the house of Proteus and Roxanna. The oracles had predicted the birth, and the child—a direct descendent of Daud—is held in awe...

31st day of Jenut, 977 YK

Acrisius and Meena have given life to Joshua Bin Acrisius, brother of Jesus Bin Acrisius. The baby is beautiful and has his father's soft eyes...he has a gentle soul...

13th day of Esau, 981 YK

The child follows his brother everywhere...their lives are one. Jesus looks at Joshua with unparalleled devotion. They're inseparable...

15th day of Daud, 984 YK

Stone turned eight today. His father Proteus is not very fond of me...Smuggling books into Shur appalls him. Much like the Elders he believes the books should remain in Nanak with the sins of the ancient world. Yet he's a noble man, and was kind enough to invite me to his home...the boy is strong for his age. He has his father's humility and his mother's regality...an uncanny charisma, and he's always smiling. He seems to have everything...he's only seven...He easily commands the attention of an audience...children flock around him...they played games...he refuses to lose...I watched him closely. I think I will for a while. He'll make a good Gatherer.

20th day of Samsara, 984 YK

Stone and Joshua met for the first time today. I watched curiously. I've been fascinated by the two boys for a while now. Joshua is quieter...Stone is more expressive. He'll have a good influence on Joshua. Joshua's father and I have been friends for many years. I see Joshua regularly...I hear that Proteus takes Stone to Council meetings. He's honing his son's skills at a young age...Jesus turns fifteen soon. We'll be initiating him at the crescent moon...

10th day of Esau, 990 YK

Joshua and Stone have become close friends...Joshua smiles when he's around Stone...He thinks a great deal. Books are his passion. ...Stone is fascinated with politics. He misses his father...He could run circles around anyone in Shur. The Elders have it coming...

14th day of Daud, 991 YK

Stone turns fifteen tomorrow. I have a difficult decision ahead of me...I wish I could initiate them both. But it is best for Shur if only one becomes a Gatherer...Maybe Joshua is the better choice.

5th day of Salman, 994 YK

I didn't accompany the Gatherers today. The tide was unusually high. They haven't returned yet. I'm concerned.

Joshua and Jesus are the best Gatherers we have. They should be all right...I must be getting old. I worry unnecessarily.

My bones have been aching. I should sleep soon.

I hope the boys are well...

6th day of Salman, 994 YK

We found the body. I held back my tears. My chest aches. I can't feel my heart anymore...I can't bear to see Joshua...They tell me that he held on to Jesus, that he tried...he felt Jesus's blood on his face...he resurfaced for air...Jesus was trapped...he couldn't remove the boulder...the water was cold...he went back below the surface to give his brother more air...his lifeless eyes...how did he feel?...dead brother...no heart...no life...they say he screamed...exhausted he couldn't continue...Jesus drowned.

On the river bank, Mehabiah wrapped Joshua up in a couple of layers to keep him warm...he refused to leave...he sat on a rock by the river with the sun setting behind him...orange sky turned dark and dire...his body shook uncontrollably...crying. I wonder if the sun will ever rise for him again.

I'm not going to date my diary anymore. I'm old. Time doesn't matter to me as much...

Joshua has not been the same. He speaks seldom and goes to Nanak often. He's been reading incessantly...carries his brother's diary with him everywhere...Jesus often spoke of a great renaissance for the people of Shur...Like me he believed in the power of education. We did, however, disagree on expanding the renaissance from the elite to the masses. He wanted us to open our teachings to the commoners. Joshua has always been interested in books and he recently spoke to me about the possibility of such a renaissance. I think he should wait. Gradual change is probably a better way to reinvent a society. I've asked him to continue using the school in my basement as a forum for debate and education. But, he doesn't think one school is enough...He's impatient...I can't blame him. How do you tell a young man that he has all the time in the world, especially when he's seen his brother die before his eyes? I wouldn't be surprised if he starts soon. It was going to happen sooner or later. Whether it was Jesus, Joshua or another Gatherer. Even though I'm skeptical about the success he'll have, I'm secretly happy. Maybe the time for discretion has passed. He shares his dreams with Catonell…The girl cares for him…I hope he doesn't love her…She fancies Stone more.

Stone has a great friend in Joshua. He has a great family; a mother and a brother who dote on him…he's fascinated by Catonell. He tells me that she's his soul mate.

I spoke with him the other day about the responsibilities of being a good leader. They can be overwhelming. Soon he'll be making decisions for the entire city and for generations of men and women. A good leader will have to make sacrifices.

But he's willing. He's chosen his position in Shur.

Stone and Catonell have been spending time together. He loves her. Catonell is a lovely girl…They're happy together…

I told him not to spend too much time at the Council Hall. He hasn't been with her much in the last few months. "I have a responsibility. She should understand," he told me. He's making his choices. He's a strong leader, but I hope he's happy also.

Joshua has started smuggling hundreds of books into Shur. He's expanded his classes from the school in my basement to almost every neighborhood in Shur. He's handing books out to whoever is interested. The Elders will find out soon. His audience is growing rapidly.

She told Stone that she didn't love him…the boys haven't told me much…I heard it from Meena. I was surprised. Women…I guess an old man like myself will never understand them either. He spoke with Joshua.

She has become a part of their past. She told Stone that she never wanted to see him again. I don't think she meant it, but he's taken it to heart. Joshua refuses to see her also.

Stone has been talking to me about Nanak…He promised Proteus that eventually they'll return….

Stone is becoming increasingly powerful…He's been coming by frequently. We discuss Shur's future…Today was his father's birthday. It has been twelve years since he died. I can tell that he misses his father. Proteus was a good influence on him…He says that he'll remove the Elders soon…He speaks of Joshua with incredible love.

The Council is becoming weary of Joshua's smuggling. He hasn't been very tactful. Hundreds of books are being brought over from Nanak during Gatherings. More statues have been desecrated with anti-religious slogans quoted from Joshua's books. The Elders are wary of Joshua's influence and the power of literature from the old world. And I can see Stone becoming impatient as well. He has spoken with Joshua already. Regardless, Joshua remains true to his utopian vision. His personal Socratic society…the naïveté of youth.

There is a prophecy about a time so grave that evil men will chase the Gatherers into the mountains. And, gradually, they will be hunted and slaughtered. I've never believed in prophecies. Joshua sometimes worries me.

The Council tried to ban Gatherings today on account of them having no practical purpose anymore—a shrewd move by Paris. Shur has been economically independent for years. I wonder how much longer they'll continue…Joshua stormed out of the meeting…Stone voted in favor of Gatherings and everyone followed suit…He spoke of the tactical importance of a continued, yet secretive presence in Nanak in case a military conquest became necessary. And he wasn't lying. Stone has been carefully studying the Gatherer routes into Nanak. He has always been interested in Nanak's geography…he even argued the inherent power of tradition. Jenut himself formed the Gatherers. Their power and duties should not be trivialized into a Council vote. The Elders could not disagree with his logic. If they argue against tradition, their argument could eventually return to haunt them.

I've never seen one man wield so much power and influence in Shur.

They found lost scriptures…anointed as the chosen one…He must go into the desert and perform three tasks. I'm weary…I have spoken to the Gatherers…Shur needs them now more than ever. Especially if Stone dies…

Stone returned today. All is well…

BOOK II:
THE KING—1008 YK–1010 YK

CHAPTER 15

❀

John the Gatherer

During Jenut's last days, on the heels of his deathbed, the Gatherers swore on the honor of Daud's God that they would always protect the city of Shur and its ideals of justice.

—*El-Theikos*, Chapter 29: Histories, verse 34

They say that mermaids never die, they only fade away. In their youth they raise their fins above the water, teasing the golden rays of Helios. But then as the years pass they hide themselves in dark caves within secluded depths, far away from the chattering of Poseidon's court. Then in the silence, they grow old and gradually become one with the ocean. The white foam on the surface of the blue sea is left behind as a reminder of their youth, and their remains nourish the ocean depths forever.

The years had passed and John was feeling his age. The deep wrinkles on his face were like erosions in the harsh, stony desert. His eyes were set deep behind his leathery brown skin and thin white eyebrows. His hands were crooked with age and his lower back was constantly aching. He wished his body was young again.

He could see Shur in the distance. He had made a journey to the mountains for meditation every year for the last thirty years. The sun was unusually harsh for this time of the year. He wiped the sand and sweat off his brow. He felt like stopping and simply lying down. He felt like disappearing into the sand. He looked up at the cloudless sky. The evening was approaching and he could see the dull white moon gradually make an appearance through the light blue sky. Soon stars would appear as well. He could not remember the last time he had stargazed.

He stopped his camel and sat in its shade. He waited for the sun god, Helios to disappear behind the sand dunes. The horizon turned orange, then red, and fizzled into a gloomy gray as the sun gradually slithered down the edge of the earth, before his deep blue eyes. A cool wind whisked away the warm lull of the scorching day as John looked up at the vast cosmos, waiting for the twinkle of glorious suns from distant galaxies. He saw the first star and smiled.

As a young man he had spent hours arguing futilely with the stars, demanding answers from the forces beyond and creating philosophical quandaries about his existence within the universe. Now, at eighty-three, he was tired of asking questions. He realized there was no God. He realized no one spoke to him. He only spoke to himself. Thus he asked no more questions. Closer to an end than to a beginning, he chose to simply enjoy.

There were times when he could sense death looming close by. Strange shadows followed him constantly. He'd turn around and they'd disappear. He knew that it was only a matter of time. Where would he go? He hoped he would go nowhere. The idea of being an atheist in a heaven crawling with believers didn't appeal to him. He didn't like their company much.

"Orion," he whispered. He searched the constellations like a fascinated child. He began counting them, but stopped after a while. The sky and the stillness of the desert had made him sleepy. He smiled, closed his eyes, and drifted into a deep slumber, scattered with dreams of youth, lost love, and glorious sadness.

❧   ❧   ❧

One would have to go a long way back to learn about John's beginnings, actually, all the way back to 955 YK, the year Samuel, leader of the Gatherers, stepped down from public service. A young man named John Tispab replaced him. The Gatherers commanded a great deal of respect from the community. Other than the practical importance of Gatherings, this obligation also arose from a fable surrounding Jenut's death that had found its way into folklore. Before taking his last breath, Jenut had anointed the Gatherers as the keepers of justice in the city. He also asked them to form a secret guild that would prevent any one Councilman from gaining absolute power and wielding a regime of corruption. He then wrote, "And the leader of the Gatherers will sit on the Council, and only his identity will remain revealed." Their symbol of unity was silence.

The folktale didn't affect the religious community much, until Samuel the Gatherer died and John was proclaimed leader of the Gatherers. The Gatherer leaders before John had been simple men, strong-limbed but feebleminded. They posed no threat to the political dominance of the Elders.

However, the potential power bestowed upon the Gatherers by Jenut was only harnessed with John's ascent on the Council. John was the first Gatherer leader with undeniable charisma. The people of Shur adored him, and when he stood up on the city column during town meetings they would cheer for him loudly. Through his articulate speech and sharp wit he would work the crowd effortlessly into hysteria, calm, or anger. His influence in the city was unquestionable. He further solidified his stature by making sure that his Gatherers entered the vital arenas of city government, the military and education; thus strategically placing them and himself at the core of city life.

According to his friends, with his power his ego grew also. When he was thirty-four, during the year 960 YK, John had become so powerful that he risked smuggling books out of Nanak into Shur. He also opened a small school in the basement of his house and, without the Elders' knowledge, he read books of the old world to a select group of people. One of such men was the soldier Acrisius, Joshua's father. Acrisius took a great liking to the Greek stories of the philosopher kings. He entered himself into John's private tutelage and worked toward strengthening his oratory skills. His power as a commanding officer, combined with the finesse of his oration, gradually made him a city favorite.

When Acrisius's skills were sufficiently honed, John conveniently took ill and couldn't make his weekly speech to the people of Shur. In his place, he sent Acrisius, who delighted the crowd with his manner and strength of words. He inspired the people with stories of the past delineating the strengths of the Shurite forefathers, beckoning the people to regain their moral individuality.

As a consequence of his public success, in the next general election Acrisius defeated the priest Cassius and was the first person in the history of Shur who was neither a priest nor from the house of Jenut to serve on the Council. A dismal clergy would soon realize that Acrisius's election was only the beginning of a pattern. Acrisius quietly recruited other capable men, and in another ten years fourteen other priests were defeated in election years.

Nevertheless, the religious grip on the city remained strong. Priests were losing elections, yet, religion was still a dominant force in government and all legal affairs. Unbeknownst to the Elders, the real blow to religious legitimacy was still a few years away.

During the year 976 YK, to the priests' dismay, Proteus, friend of Acrisius, the son of Perseus, the father of Stone, from the house of Jenut, began visiting John's secret sessions. He was seen entering and leaving John's house with Acrisius during the dark hours of the night. Alongside him, other prominent figures were also spotted.

In the eyes of the clergy, the corruption of the political elite had begun with books written by Nietzsche, Locke, Plato, and Rousseau; encouraging them toward creating non-religious systems, and rebelling against archetypes. The influence of these books was felt in the Council, as a small group of prominent city leaders began suggesting secular systems of government.

However, the priests, under Paris' steady leadership, responded quickly. They skimmed through *El-Theikos* with a fine-tooth comb and found verses in numerous chapters that condemned the learnings and ways of the ancient world. These chapters were distributed during religious sermons. People were encouraged to destroy any books that had come over through the negligence or ignorance of the Gatherers. The Shurite mob was disturbed by the harrowing sermons, which triggered fears of eternal damnation. They were reminded of God's wrath and the manner in which an entire world had been destroyed, while only a few deserving children had been spared.

John recognized the genuine concern of the Shurites. He knew that they were not ready for a complete reeducation, and so he cut back significantly on his personal renaissance. In one of his greatest and most effective speeches he assured the people that the only books he had smuggled out of Nanak were instructions on military tactics. He had done so to prevent the Nanakites from accumulating an unfair advantage in military strength. Not only had he smuggled all these books out of Nanak, he had also destroyed at least one hundred military texts, and would do the same during every Gathering. He turned away from the people and pointed across the river to the Nanakite skyline. "And you will see smoke rising into the skies before I return home."

He kept his promise. During every Gathering he would prepare a small fire and, instead of books, he would burn dry leaves on the riverbanks. The people in Shur would see the smoke rise into the sky and cheer for John the Gatherer.

Nevertheless, John carefully recruited pupils and opened their minds to new ideas, slowly destroying the cage of moral obligations that dominated their daily decisions. Once free, he wanted them to search for mores and principles within his books. As most self-professed atheists, John replaced God with a search for the ultimate truth—a truth that in his mind would rebuke the possibility of nothingness. Naturally he didn't rule out the possibility of nothingness. He only hoped that the opposite was true. Sometimes, he suspected that his search would essentially validate his fear of a purposeless, nihilistic existence. Yet deep in his core, he also felt that if he maintained his resolve he could find the one thread that tied everything together and ultimately explained the cosmos. A complete destruction of nihilism and religious theology: a pure truth without God.

He shared his thoughts freely with his Gatherers and encouraged debate and discussion amongst them. For many years, late during Gatherings, John would take his men into the libraries of Nanak and they would go through two books at a time. By the time John was sixty-five, every living Gatherer was versed in political, religious, and philosophical thought. He was pleased that he had presented strong men with strong minds.

Despite the learnings of the old world, many of his pupils remained true to their religion. One of such pupils was Proteus. Even though he tried to revise outdated and archaic religious laws, he didn't deviate from the essential doctrines of religious and eternal prosperity. John didn't mind his pupil's faith in God. After all, he knew that each man had to find his own truth.

As a part of his religious rituals, Proteus visited the temples regularly, and during his visits the priests desperately tried to influence his thoughts. Eventually he took their religious warnings to heart. He looked through *El-Theikos* and found verses that condemned the old world. He read the verses from numerous angles and dissected them thoroughly, and was finally convinced that God had destroyed the old world because of its sinful ways. An extremely pious man, Proteus gradually broke from John's path. In the year 980 YK, Proteus made the separation official during a Council session by announcing that any secret meetings over philosophical materials that may cause political disturbances in the city would be condemned by the house of Jenut. The priests cheered him along as he put forth a passionate speech presenting the importance of religion and God. With tears in his eyes, Proteus looked at the Council and beckoned them to commit themselves to God, who in good time would unveil all truths.

John appreciated Proteus's faith in God, but his emphatic religious endorsement made it difficult for him to continue with his teachings. More importantly, Proteus's son Stone was getting older, and John sensed a unique greatness in him. He wanted the child as a pupil. But Proteus made every attempt to keep the child away from John.

Proteus, an adroit politician, began polishing Stone's political skills at an early age. The child accompanied his father to Council meetings when he was only five. Proteus was constantly showering the boy with political advice, warning him of possible pitfalls and encouraging him toward gymnastics and military prowess. The boy was strong and sharp by the time he was ten.

In 988 YK, when Stone was twelve, Proteus was struck by consumption. After struggling admirably against the disease, he gave way to mortality during a cold, harsh winter. The city had lost a great son and the priests a great ally.

Acrisius, Proteus's best friend and confidant, became Stone's legal guardian, and thus John entered Stone's life. John and Stone met on the riverbank. John showed him how to skip stones off of the river. In the next few years, John taught him many more things. He further sharpened Stone's political prowess and added a philosophical dimension to his personality. With a plethora of strengths and weapons, Stone became the youngest person ever elected to the Shurite Council. He was only seventeen.

With Stone educated and the Gatherers enlightened, John retired from public life in the year 1002. His retirement was followed by Joshua's anointment as leader of the Gatherers, which surprised most Shurites. Everyone had thought that Stone was a Gatherer and thus they had expected him to take over John's seat in the Council. But John had not recruited Stone to be a Gatherer. He wanted to keep the scales balanced.

Joshua was very popular amongst his peers and his Elders. But he had always been Jesus' younger brother. Hidden away in Jesus' shadow, the city had never recognized his strengths. However, after Jesus' death, Joshua had been pushed into the limelight of the city's political arena. He responded to his fate by effortlessly filling both Jesus's and John's shoes, whether it was in debate, speech, or political battles. Acrisius was not surprised. He had always known of Joshua's abilities.

Joshua's appointment to the Council, however, was followed by another harrowing tragedy. Acrisius awoke late one night dreaming of his son Jesus. Drenched in sweat, he ran out of his house into the street. Joshua followed him out. Acrisius kept repeating Jesus' name, looking for him, trying to save him. Then he fell on the street. His heart had failed him.

His funeral was held in the Main Temple at the center of the city, beside City Hall. Joshua's eulogy was short and beautiful. Sitting in the crowd, John the Gatherer looked around at all the young faces, searching for old friends, realizing that they were dwindling and that soon he wouldn't find any. He felt sad, but then he caught a glimpse of Stone. He turned his eyes back to Joshua. He watched Joshua walk away from the pulpit. Joshua stopped next to Stone and embraced him.

"A new world," John thought to himself as the feeling of sadness gave way to that of hope.

❦   ❦   ❦

Joshua looked out of the attic window. He could see the river, and the moon looming above it. He could smell the morning air whisking in, pushing aside the dry lou of the previous night. He rubbed his eyes and tried to stay awake. He realized that he hadn't slept for days. The last few nights he'd been working with Stone at the Capitol, preparing for the upcoming coronation.

"Joshua!" his mother shouted his name from downstairs.

"Yes, Mother," Joshua replied.

"Are you going for your walk today?"

"In a while."

"Could you bring me some milk from your sister's place?"

"I will."

"Don't forget," she said. "I need it for dinner."

"I won't."

Joshua walked downstairs out through the front door into the cool summer morning. He took in a deep breath and looked around. The streets were bare. Everyone was still asleep.

He walked alongside the river, away from the city toward the desert. Here on the edge of the city, every morning, he would watch the sun rise. He sat on his usual rock and looked at the yellow sand as it stretched out toward the Kalabaash Mountains. The sky tightly wrapped his world together, touching both the city behind him and the great mountains before him. The night was clear and the stars numerous.

Gradually, the moon began fading, as the dark night yielded to a light gray and the stars receded into the endless cosmos. He could see the sun gradually peek over the horizon. In a few moments the mountains were consumed by fire. The bright orange of the morning sun danced passionately with shades of red, yellow, and blue. Every object in the cosmos was bleeding color, and for a while Joshua couldn't tell the heavens and the earth apart—they were consumed by a passionate dance at the edge of the world.

The sky was now a light orange. The reds and yellows were fading away into a pale blue. Joshua stared at the sun. His eyelids were heavy. He could barely keep them open. He closed his eyes. The world stopped around him, and he thought he was asleep.

"Mister?"

Joshua turned around. A boy stood before him.

"Mister," the boy said. "You're standing on my toy."

"Oh," Joshua said. "I'm sorry." He stepped aside.

The boy picked up his toy and walked toward the river.

"Hello," Joshua said.

The boy turned around and smiled, "Hello."

"Are you here alone?"

"Yes."

"Where are your parents?" Joshua asked.

"They're asleep."

"Do they know that you're...?"

"Have you been there?" the boy interrupted as he pointed to Nanak.

Joshua was silent.

"I know who you are," the boy said to Joshua.

"Who am I?"

"You're Joshua the Gatherer," the boy said. "My father talks about you."

"What's his name?"

"Have you been to Nanak?" the boy asked, avoiding Joshua's question.

"Yes, I have," Joshua replied.

"How is it?"

"It's beautiful," Joshua said. "Great libraries, and great schools."

Joshua and the boy gazed at Nanak.

"Are the people nice?" the boy asked.

"Yes," Joshua said.

"My father says they must be."

"Why does he say that?"

"Because you stay there for so long when you go."

Joshua smiled.

"Where are all your friends?" Joshua asked.

"They're asleep," the boy said.

"At least you don't have to go to school today."

"I don't like school."

"Nobody does," Joshua said.

"You didn't like school?" the boy asked.

"That's right."

"Did you have many friends?" the boy asked.

"A few," Joshua said.

"Who's your best friend?" the boy asked.

"My brother."

"But he died."

"Who told you about that?" Joshua asked.

The boy was quiet. He knew he had spoken without thinking. "Everyone knows," he mumbled softly.

"He died over there," Joshua pointed. "He got trapped close to the bridge and got pulled under."

"I have no brothers."

"Do you have any siblings?" Joshua asked.

"No," the boy replied. "So who're your friends now?"

"Stone is one of my friends."

"When did you meet?" the boy asked.

"We were very young," Joshua replied.

"Is he your best friend now?" the boy asked.

"Yes."

"My father says it's good that you and Stone are friends."

"He does?"

"Yes," the boy said. "He says if you were not friends there would be a great war."

"Why does he think that?"

"He says that Stone is not a Gatherer," the boy said.

"How does he know?"

"He knows," the boy said. "Everyone knows."

"Okay," Joshua said.

"He also says the Gatherers are the only people Stone will never have power over," the boy said. "So it's good that you two are friends, because if you weren't Stone would find and kill all the Gatherers."

Joshua started laughing.

"He wouldn't do that," Joshua said.

"That's what my father says."

"You always listen to what he says?"

"I go with my father to the Council meetings."

"What's his name?"

"He doesn't have a name," the boy looked away.

"Why doesn't your father have a name?" Joshua asked.

"He just doesn't," the boy replied.

"Okay," Joshua said. "What's your name?"

"I am Manu," the boy smiled. "The one who cuts and measures."

"You have a long name," Joshua said.

"Yes it is," the boy replied. "Will you ever be king?"

"No," Joshua said. "That's an odd question."

"Why not?" the boy asked.

"Because Stone is king,"

"That doesn't mean that you can't be King."

"Actually it does," Joshua said. "And I don't want to be King."

The boy started humming to himself.

"What time do you think it is?" he asked.

"It should be six."

"Are you awake or are you asleep?" the boy asked.

"What?" Joshua said bewildered.

The boy looked at the sun nervously, as if he was late for something.

"I have to go now," he said.

"Why?"

The boy stood up with his toy in his hand and ran toward the city. Joshua lifted his hand to wave.

The boy stopped and looked back at Joshua. The orange sun made his hair look red.

"Don't let them take your books away," the boy said.

"What did you say?"

"Your books," the boy said. "Don't let them take your books."

He turned around and ran away.

CHAPTER 16

❀

Roxanna

Beware a mother's vengeance, for its fire breathes heavier than any flames in hell.

—*El-Theikos*, Chapter 554: Children, verse 76

Roxanna walked through the dark alley in the quietest part of town. Her head and face were covered. She walked by a few deserted homes and disappeared into the uninhabited maze of ancient Shur. Deep in the thicket of condemned edifices, she heard a voice whisper to her.

"Roxanna."

She stopped and turned toward the voice.

"Paris," she whispered. "Is that you?"

"Yes."

Paris appeared from the shadows. She removed the veil from her face. He looked at her and thought back thirty years to the first time he had noticed her in the Council Hall. She was a stunning woman. She had come to see Proteus. Only beautiful women came to see him.

"This is a good time," she said. "Joshua's busy with the Council."

"What did you want to talk about?" Paris asked.

"He could become a liability," she said. "I want to know where you stand."

"Let's go inside and talk."

"Like old friends," she smiled wryly, thinking about the day she had first approached him thirty years ago. "Undermine John," she had said. "For he shall never share glory with Proteus." That day a strange pairing had occurred. Paris and Roxanna, despite their mutual dislike for each other, found themselves in harmony. They had met covertly several times in the following years. The term "old friends" was still echoing in his mind as they walked into the dark building.

"More like old villains," he replied.

She thought about his comment. Maybe she had been a villain a few times in the past, but when it came to protecting her husband and her son, she didn't mind playing the part.

CHAPTER 17

❀

Coronation

Then Daud took a flask of oil and poured it on Zamin's head and kissed him saying "Has not the Lord anointed you leader of his inheritance."

—*El-Theikos*, Chapter 322: Kings, verse 1

Many years ago, in the harshest regions of the desert, a caravan was stranded. The shadows of the mountains devoured the caravan as a storm of hail and fire struck every inch of the muddy earth. The men couldn't see much, and the moon hid far away behind the black clouds that shrouded the evening sky. Their camels were exhausted and their bodies were bruised. The annual visit to the mountains for oil had turned into a confrontation with a small band of Nanakites. The men had engaged each other, and after losing six Shurites, Stone's caravan had fled from the mountains toward the city. The Nanakites were in pursuit, but under Stone's guidance the Shurites had created a substantial distance between themselves and the Nanakites.

Yet Nahum's camel had died, and Jonathan's horse could not move. They had left the animals behind. But the losses had slowed the caravan considerably.

"Alaaaaaaaaayyyyy," the rider in the back shouted, pointing toward a black spot in the distance that moved closer to the men and grew larger with every passing moment.

"They're closing in," Mehabiah said.

"We'll be fine," Stone said.

"What happens if we don't reach the city?"

"We'll be fine," Stone said again as he signaled for the caravan to move faster. Then he stopped his horse and turned it around. The men stopped their camels.

"Keep moving!" Stone shouted. His horse danced around in one spot as lightning lit up the skies behind him. The camel riders could see only his outline against the angry sky.

Mehabiah rode his horse toward Stone.

"What are you doing?"

"Keep moving, Mehabiah," Stone said. "And don't let the caravan stop!"

"What are you doing?" Mehabiah asked again.

"Keep the caravan moving," Stone said again.

Mehabiah turned his horse around and galloped to the front of the caravan. He signaled the caravan to follow him. Stone waited for the caravan to pass. Then he drew his sword and rode his horse furiously toward the Nanakites.

Mehabiah froze for a moment. He could see Stone become smaller as he rode away from the caravan toward the black spot in the distance.

The Shurites stopped.

"No!" Mehabiah shouted. "Follow me!"

The men were bewildered.

"He told us to keep moving," Mehabiah said.

The men did not move.

"He told us to keep moving!" he shouted again.

The men slowly nudged their camels toward Mehabiah, and with their eyes still fixed on Stone, reluctantly followed the trail back to Shur.

They could no longer see Stone. The black spot was still behind them, but it wasn't getting any larger. Then after a few moments, it started moving westward away from the caravan. Arjuna rode his camel toward Mehabiah.

"He's taking them away from us," Mehabiah said.

"How'll he catch up?" Arjuna asked.

"He will."

The caravan moved swiftly toward Shur, and as the storm gave way to clear skies the Shurites entered the safety of their refugee city.

Early the next morning, Stone returned. His right arm was broken. His left eye was swollen shut and a deep gash ran across his forehead an inch above his brow.

A few days later the Gatherer's returned from Nanak, where Joshua, while in the Nanakite marketplace, had heard a story of a Mad Horseman who had single-

handedly engaged an army of Nanakites, leading them on a wild goose chase through the stony cliffs and hazardous rocks of Kalabaash.

Such stories about Stone were common. He smiled when he looked around at the crowd congregated in the temple.

"Should we begin?" Paris whispered.

Stone nodded his head. He was surrounded by hundreds of people who stood cramped in the large hall. The temple was grand. High ceilings, wide stairs leading to the throne, exquisitely decorated pillars, and large windows evoked the grandeur of divinity.

The coronation began with a clergy hymn. Stone looked at Joshua, who stood in front of the crowd. Joshua was thinking about his conversation with Manu. He was still confused. He wasn't sure if the boy had appeared to him in a dream or if he had actually spoken to him. He had asked around about the child, but no one seemed to know of his parents or of his family. Joshua shrugged his thoughts aside and decided to pay attention to the coronation. He looked at Stone and felt good about Shur's future. His ascent into glory was a journey of small, calculated steps, marked by some small and some monumental sacrifices.

"It'll be difficult," John had said.

"I'll be fine."

"Are you happy?"

"I have everything," he had replied. "Why wouldn't I be happy?"

"Can you throw it all away for the good of the people?"

"Everything?"

"Yes," John had said. "Everything."

"I can," he had said, after pondering the question for a while.

"Even Catonell?" John had asked.

Stone had not answered his question. He wasn't sure then. Yet both John and Joshua knew that Stone was strong enough to change Shur, and he would sacrifice everything, if needed, for a greater future.

Joshua looked at Stone on Jenut's throne, and hoped that he was truly happy with the path he had deliberately chosen. Joshua then turned his gaze toward the people and wondered if they realized that the coronation was only a symbolic event, officially recognizing the power Stone had assumed a long time ago.

＊   ＊   ＊

Following the coronation, Stone spoke with Joshua about the desecrated statues and the latest rumors of anti-religious Gatherings. Many of the basic reading sessions had given way to revolutionary meetings. According to Council spies, the readings taunted God and religion. Paris claimed that Pan, the god of mischief, had taken over the proceedings, and a slew of vile incidents had been witnessed during the night. Joshua refused to believe Paris's accusations. He couldn't imagine his books causing a stir so great and his students abusing the gospel.

Despite knowing that some of the more controversial books were missing from his library, Joshua tempered Stone's concerns about the anti-government graffiti that had been sprayed on holy statues around the city.

Stone secretly wondered if Joshua's books were causing a disruption of the society he planned to mold. John had once told him, "Molding an ignorant mind is much easier than molding a mind influenced by knowledge." Regardless, Stone allowed Joshua to rectify the situation, yet deep in his heart he knew that censorship was necessary.

"They'll listen to me," Joshua said. "I'll ask them to stop."

"I know you will," Stone replied confidently.

CHAPTER 18

❀

Manu

I looked up at the clouds and a spirit was coming, headfirst like arrows slanting down; and as he came, he sang a sacred song and the thunder was like drumming. I will sing the song for you. "Behold a sacred voice is calling you; all over the sky a sacred voice is calling you."

—*El-Theikos*, Chapter 248: Jenut, verses 7 8

The child had a strange face. It was the face of a man with old eyes. Joshua would shudder in his sleep when the child's face appeared. There was something mysteriously frightening about him—enough so that Joshua would deliberately break himself from his dreams. There were even times during the day, while wide awake, that Joshua would see the boy, sometimes in the marketplace and sometimes at the Council. He would follow the child but would soon lose him around a corner or in an alley. The last time the child had led him into a chance meeting with Paris.

He had looked around a surprised Paris to see if the boy was behind him. Soon afterward he had checked the Shurite archives and a child by the name of Manu did not exist in Shur. Maybe it was a nickname. Yet it was odd that he would see this child sporadically in the marketplace and almost every night in his dreams. He mentioned his illusions to his mother. She advised him to seek out an oracle. But he didn't believe in or trust oracles; usually they were high ranking priests and Council members.

"I think the child's an omen," his mother said. "You should go see Fatima. She's not a Council member. And she has no friends. She'll keep your secrets."

Joshua thought about his mother's suggestion, but then dismissed the idea. He didn't believe in omens or supernatural signs. He knew his mind was playing tricks on him. He also took solace in the fact that his grandfather had had illusions as well. His were, however, far more disturbing than Joshua's.

With Manu's appearance, Joshua was now more curious about his grandfather's insanity. His mother reluctantly told him the story. Grandfather Ibrahim would see strange green people appearing out of dark alleys. In crowded streets, he would start screaming and tearing his hair out. Eventually, the family had to lock him up in a room. They found him dead the next morning. His fingernails were eroded and his skull was crushed. The little people in his mind were so real and the escape so necessary, he had tried to dig his way out of the room from under one of the walls. His head got trapped under the wall. He had almost escaped.

Joshua felt strangely relieved. In a sense he preferred madness over the supernatural. After all, if Manu was real then another dimension of reality existed and Joshua's theories about the afterlife would crumble. He liked believing that different dimensions were foolish dreams. He liked the mortality of his life, which in turn encouraged him toward living immaculately, searching for the ultimate truth in every single moment.

Despite his assertions about oracles and the supernatural, Joshua's curiosity led him to Fatima. She lived in an old shack in ancient Shur. The shack had been built on top of a skyscraper. Joshua climbed thirty flights of stairs. It was dark. Nobody else lived in the colossal building. The silence and darkness added to the morbidity, and the time it took to reach the summit compounded his fears.

Once he reached the summit he knocked on her door twice. A booming echo followed his knock. He waited for a while. He could hear her unlock the door. She was a thin old lady. He followed her into her home. Except for the glow of a lantern in the middle of her living room, her home was dark. Books covered every wall. She asked him to sit down. She didn't talk much.

"Tell me about the boy," she asked.

He told her everything.

She went into a back room. He waited for her. She returned with a book and flipped through a few pages.

"Here it is," she said.

Joshua was curious. He leaned forward. A picture of an angel was on one page and on the opposite page was the image of a demon.

"The name of the child is Manu."

Joshua waited for her to speak again.

"Did you see him in a dream?" she asked.

"I was at the river," Joshua said. "I don't remember. I may have been asleep. It was late and I was tired."

"Manu is the angel of fate," she said. "He shows in many forms. He can show himself as an angel or as a demon."

"Fate?" Joshua asked. "What does he want with me?"

"You never know about these things," she said. "He might want to tell you something. Listen to him. Listen to what he says, and maybe he'll tell you what he wants."

Joshua, forever the compassionate skeptic, nodded his head politely.

"Do you believe in fate, Joshua?" the lady asked.

Joshua thought about her question for a few seconds.

"I'm not sure if I do," he replied.

CHAPTER 19

❀

Memories

O God, do not keep silent; be not quiet, be not still. O God, see how your enemies are astir, how your foes rear their heads. With cunning they conspire against your people, they plot against those you cherish.

—*El-Theikos*, Chapter 74: Prayer, verses 1–3

The clown cried, and the children laughed. Stone smiled. The monkey pounded on the harmonium creating grotesque disfigured sounds. Stone winced. He didn't like carnivals. They were too loud. The clown danced around, and the children screamed as he approached them. A small child in the front row turned and ran into his mother's arms. The fat man behind the donkey played his drums louder, and the clown sang an old nursery rhyme, his big yellow teeth and purple tongue on stage for the world.

"Catonell."

Stone turned around. "Where?" he thought. Had he heard her name? He searched the crowd. He couldn't see her. He had been thinking about her again. Maybe he had shouted out her name in his head.

"Get outta the way!" the clown shouted.

He pushed Stone aside and laughed. The children were silent. The clown was surprised. He turned around and looked at Stone.

"Forgive me," he said, "I didn't recognize…"

It had been six days since the coronation and the clown was embarrassed. He continued to apologize. Stone didn't want the children's party to end. He patted the clown on the back and pushed him back into the scene with the monkey, the donkey, and the fat man. The carnival continued.

"Catonell," he thought. He smiled.

He loved her more now than he had the day she broke his heart. He had never felt a pain so deep. He would think about her and remember her smell. He would see her eyes and remember the endless hours of bliss he had spent with her. He would think and he would remember because, like any emotion, his love for her was an experience—a memory of a boy standing in a dark room during the early hours of the morning wondering why he had rushed to save a potted plant, wondering why his reflexes had beckoned him to protect a gift from a special girl, and in doing so realizing the extent of his love for her and the extent to which she had become a part of him.

Many years ago, he had awoken to a crashing sound. He found himself standing beside his window looking at the plant she had given him. The plant was from John's greenhouse. She knew that it was Stone's favorite plant, and she knew that John grew the flower in his garden.

"You'll have to nurture it from a sapling," John had told her.

She agreed. She spent an hour every day after school in the greenhouse for six months and made sure that the plant was strong. Then she presented it to Stone. He loved the gift. He had kept it with him constantly. But after she broke his heart, he stopped watering the plant and eventually he threw it away.

"Stupid boy," he thought to himself with a smile. Sometimes he felt like throwing her memories away as well. But he had loved her so much that he simply couldn't. Thus, he decided to keep her tucked away in his mind like a favorite record. Once in a while he would run through their memories, one song after another, sad songs intermingled with happy ones. He knew that as he grew older, and as he inevitably distanced himself from their emotions and experiences, his memories would fade into timeworn lyrics. And eventually the remnants of their love would be replaced by the static of an old record scratching against an even older needle, because even the most beautiful songs are often forgotten.

＊   ＊   ＊

John did not remember when he first started talking to himself. He told himself to remain silent. The Council had presided before him. Fifty-four men had taken their seats. Stone sat at the front facing the Councilmen. It was his first Council meeting after the coronation. He looked like a king in his robes.

"He would look like a king even if he wore rags," John thought to himself.

John turned his head toward the contingency of Elders sitting in the right corner of the Council Hall. Ahab stroked his golden cane with one hand and twirled his beard with the other. Paris stared straight ahead at Stone. Paris turned around slowly and caught John's eye. Both men stared at each other. They smiled. Countless memories stormed through their minds within the few seconds in which they held each other's gaze. Countless battles had been waged between the two men.

"They're mine," John seemed to say silently.

"I'll have this one," Paris replied with a twisted smile.

"No, you won't."

"All in good time."

Their silence was interrupted by Stone's gavel. The meeting was in order. John slowly walked around behind the pillars, which separated him from the Council floor. He wanted a glimpse of Joshua.

"In black," John whispered softly. He was speaking to himself again.

"Old men always speak to themselves," he said softly.

"Our friends die, and we have no one else to speak to," he said.

"And the children…they ignore the old, or they want to learn from them," he said.

"They don't want to be friends," he said.

Joshua's voice interrupted John's conversation with himself, and for a moment John was coming back from a long way away. He pushed aside his tired thoughts and tuned himself into the present moment. Paris had inquired about the Gatherers.

"But he is chosen by God," Paris said.

"I know," Joshua replied.

"Then tell him the names of the Gatherers."

The Councilmen stirred in their seats. Their voices muffled and echoed off of the Council walls. Stone struck his gavel. Everyone was silent again.

"I cannot," Joshua said to Paris's request.

"You don't trust God?" Paris asked.

The Council Hall was silent. Ahab broke the silence.

"Ha!" Ahab yelped from the corner.

The Councilmen began mumbling to one another once again. "How can he?" "Why are they?" "Why is he?" "But Joshua doesn't believe." "Gatherers." "Joshua's a good man." "Keepers of justice…"

Stone struck his gavel again.

"I ask the Council to remain silent," Stone said firmly.

Everyone was silent.

"I have taken an oath," Joshua replied. "The people of Shur will always be protected by the Gatherers, but they will never know their names."

"But we have a King now."

"Jenut said that the Gatherers must remain silent," said Joshua.

"Until the Chosen arrived," said Paris.

"He did not say that," Joshua said.

"Do you believe that Stone is chosen by God?" Paris asked.

In half a second, with his eyes only, and without moving his head, Joshua swiftly looked around the Council room. He caught John staring at him. John nodded.

"Yes," Joshua replied.

"Do you really?"

"Why, Paris?" Joshua replied. "Do you have doubts?"

"I anointed him," said Paris.

"That you did," said Joshua.

"You think you can protect him with a group of men he doesn't know."

"With a group of men you don't know," said Joshua.

Paris looked visibly shaken by Joshua's answer.

"Are you accusing me of something, Joshua?"

"No," Joshua said. "Of course not."

"I baptized him, and I anointed him!" Paris said firmly.

Joshua did not respond. The Council Hall was silent.

"And for now, I have nothing more to say," Paris said. "I'd like to table the conversation."

Stone looked at Joshua.

"I have no opposition to Paris's proposal," Joshua said.

"Then I concede the floor to Councilmen Ahab," Paris said.

The battle was over for the moment.

"Is that all?" Joshua asked.

"Yes," Stone replied. "Ahab, you can present your proposal now."

Ahab stood up and presented a minor city ordinance proposal dealing with the sewage system. The Council discussed the issue. Joshua walked to Stone's chair and asked his leave. He kissed Stone's hand and walked down the aisle, which separated the Elders from the rest of the Council. His robes brushed by Paris. Paris grabbed Joshua's robes gently. Joshua stopped. Paris gestured him to come closer. Joshua's ear was close to Paris's lips.

"I will anoint you with your blood," said Paris with a smile.

"I'm sure you will," Joshua replied.

CHAPTER 20

❀

The Gatherer

Rescue my sons, O Lord from evil men; protect them from men of violence who devise evil plans in their hearts. Who chase these Gatherers from their cities into the mountains.

—*El-Theikos*, Chapter 2: Daud, verse 1

When they were young, the two boys were always on the same team. Joshua always picked Stone, and Stone always picked Joshua. Other than a genuine affection for each other, their choices had much to do with their personal dispositions—they didn't like losing. The only time both boys faced each other the game ended in a tie and Joshua was taken home on a stretcher. He took a knee to the face while Stone tried to score a goal. Stone himself lost a bone chip in his right leg, and even as a man he struggled during rigorous army drills. After a long day of exercise he would start limping. He desperately disguised the limp in an effort to conceal his weakness. Yet only Joshua could see Stone limp. And in those moments, only Stone could see Joshua's slightly disfigured jaw, caused by the childhood injury. The men would smile at each other. They knew each other better than they knew themselves.

From that day on, their mothers forbade them to play against each other, which upset the other boys on the street. The decision was debated for many months. Yet a mother's word, especially concerning her child, usually is, and almost always should be taken seriously. And so for the rest of their young lives, Joshua and Stone played on the same team, and always won. The two boys didn't think they could ever lose, and they loved each other's company because, among other things, they associated their successes with their union. They were inseparable.

"You were inseparable as children," John said.

John lay on his bed. His thin, lifeless body covered with white sheets. The room was dark. Joshua walked toward the mantle and lit another candle.

"Open the windows, Joshua," John said weakly.

Joshua opened the windows.

"Ah, the fresh air of a summer night," John said.

Stone stood up and walked to the window, and gazed at the sky.

"I wish it didn't have to end," John said.

Joshua walked to John's bed.

"How do you feel, John?"

John started coughing. Stone turned away from the window and gave John a glass of water.

"I feel very weak," John said. "And you?"

"I feel fine,"

"Stone," John said.

"Yes, John," Stone replied.

"How are you, my boy?" John asked.

"I'm doing fine, John," he said.

"Make sure to get your rest," John said. "Remember, you're thinking for them now, too."

"Don't worry," Stone said.

"I wish for peace," John said with a sad smile. "I never thought I'd be sad."

John closed his eyes. His breathing was heavier. He shook for a second and sat up as if awaking from a dream.

"Stay together," he said softly.

His body slowly wilted back onto the bed. He lay motionless for a moment. Then he took a deep, final breath. His lungs lifted slightly. The air left his open mouth, as life escaped his body.

"What?" Joshua asked. "What did he say, Stone?"

"I don't know."

Joshua held his hand tightly. Stone's eyes teared up. He quickly wiped the tears away. He walked around the bed and put his hand on Joshua's shoulder. Both men were quiet. Their teacher had died. A cricket drowned the silence in the background. The stars were still shining.

"I'll bring in the rest," Stone said.

Joshua nodded his head.

Stone walked to the door and opened it. Their families, and other well-wishers from Shur congregated in the hall outside. Stone nodded his head as everyone lined up and paid their final respects to John the Gatherer.

      ✿   ✿   ✿

His mind was like a maze cluttered with dead ends, each reflecting a painful loss or a regrettable decision. Trapped in his own mistakes, like a pendulum sustained by perpetual motion, his present actions only added more fuel to the fire of regrets that had consumed his life.

Late at night, all alone, his pain would become unbearable and in his mind's eyes his inadequacies were magnified. Most nights, a heavy weight would settle on his chest and he would turn in his bed until dawn. When he was ready to sleep it was too late, and he would have to rise for another day.

"God, no!" he shouted in the dark as he sat up in his bed, drenched in his sweat. He held his head in his hands, and rubbed his temples in a futile attempt to erase the painful images from his mind.

"Why?" he asked. "I tried to do everything right."

He would then talk to God. In his mind he would open a small door to salvation and God would hold his hand and forgive his misdeeds. "You're doing this in my name," God would say. "Feel no guilt, feel no remorse."

He walked away from his bed into the side room, where he kept his flowers. He felt peaceful in his garden. He watered some of the plants and made sure that each one was taken care of properly. As he worked on his garden he mulled over the day and over John's death. He had outlived the old Gatherer.

He had outlived everyone. They had always thought of him as a runt, a pest amongst kings. They had laughed at him during army drills, and they had pushed him around in the Council. He had hated Joshua's father. Acrisius had made a profession out of embarrassing him during Council meetings. He had always thought of Acrisius as arrogant and contemptuous. He had lost many close votes because of Acrisius's pedantry.

As he watered his plants, he remembered festering with anger in dark corners, vowing vengeance and squinting at every heckle of the booming laughter directed toward him. To overcome his inadequacies, he had worked harder and he had run longer every day so that he could match swords with Acrisius, but ultimately he would always lose. He would stay up late thinking of retorts to

Acrisius's attacks, but he could never think of enough, and his frustrations were deepened because charisma and strength didn't come to him naturally. Why had God denied him charm and bestowed his enemy with it instead?

"Why didn't you like me?" he thought.

As he stepped outside onto the balcony, he looked up at the skies.

"Where are you now?" he asked.

"We're dead, Paris," the skies answered silently.

Paris laughed.

"Yes," he said. "You sure are."

CHAPTER 21

❀

Funeral

And my soul is consumed with a longing for something other than nothing.

—*El-Theikos*, Chapter 489: The Atheist, verse 34

The streets were silent, and everyone wore black. It was a cold, somber morning. The sun hid behind dark clouds and mist covered the cobbled path. Joshua felt a raindrop on his forehead. He looked up at the sky. He dragged himself along with the funeral procession. Stone and three other Councilmen carried John's body. Joshua strolled behind them and realized that he felt almost nothing. He knew that John was dead and he knew that circumstances in Shur would change as a result of his friend's death, but still he didn't really feel anything. After all, John simply didn't exist anymore, and one day he too would not exist, and everything meant nothing anyway, so why should anyone feel anything.

Realizing his lack of humanity, Joshua tried to feel sad, but he simply couldn't. He looked at everyone else and realized that they cried for selfish reasons. They cried because John's death created a vacuum in their lives. Joshua's heart didn't feel empty. It just felt heavy. He was tired. He was tired of societal standards, and he wanted to escape. John would have laughed at the funeral and its attendants. Why wasn't his body just dumped away with the rest of the trash? It was only an empty, dead vessel. John had become nothing, and you cannot bury or say goodbye to nothing.

The thunder brought Joshua back into the world, away from his morbid subconscious. He looked at John's corpse. He was gone. Why had he been born? It was a matter of chance. By chance he was able to live, and now after eighty-five years his chance to experience the world and all of its addictive, amorous, overwhelming, intoxicating, ecstatic pleasures was over. His capsule of time—eighty four years within millions—had expired. He was gone. And millions of years would aimlessly follow after him. If life meant nothing and there was no purpose, then John being born was a miracle in itself. And so for the first time during the funeral, as Joshua realized that his mentor had lost the precious gift of finite life, he felt sad, and even though no one could really tell, a tear flowed over and trickled down his cheek. The rain concealed it well.

❧   ❧   ❧

"When was the last time you saw Catonell?" Mehabiah asked.

"A couple of days," Joshua replied from the hammock in Mehabiah's court-yard.

"How is it?" Mehabiah asked. He lay on the courtyard floor looking up at the sky.

"It's strange," Joshua replied. "It's like talking to my past."

"Is the friendship still there?"

Joshua was silent. He smiled sadly.

"I think so," he said. "We used to be close."

"Does it make you sad?"

"I'm not sure," Joshua said. "I'm not sure if I really care."

"You care," Mehabiah said.

"Does it really matter?"

"I think it depends," Mehabiah said.

"Elaborate."

"Is she worth it?"

Joshua paused and thought about Mehabiah's question. He was picturing Catonell when they were younger. He thought back to a time when she had loved Stone, and the day she had hurt him. He remembered the look of despair on Stone's face, and his struggle to conceal the piercing pain that tore through his heart. Joshua had never seen Stone vulnerable before.

He had taken Stone into a temple. He didn't want anyone to see Stone weak. As both men sat in the pews of the temple, Stone's face in his hands, Joshua recognized the unrealistic expectations that had always been saddled on Stone's shoulders. Even Joshua was guilty of preserving Stone's infallibility. He wondered if in the darkest corners of Stone's conscience there existed pure unadulterated pain. Did the pain yearn for escape? Did it shred his body and soul?

Things could have ended differently if Catonell had been more patient. She had tried to meet with Stone a few years after the betrayal, but he refused to see her. He had exiled her from his life, even though Joshua suspected that she often occupied and haunted his mind.

"So?" Mehabiah asked.

"What?" Joshua said.

"You didn't answer my question."

"I'm sorry," Joshua said. "What was it again?"

"Is she worth it?" Mehabiah repeated the question.

"Once," Joshua replied. "I think she was."

CHAPTER 22

❀

Reeducation

It is the glory of God to conceal a matter. To search out a matter is the glory of man.

—*El-Theikos*, Chapter 646: Proverbs, verse 34

Joshua looked out at John's lighthouse from a window in the Council Hall. The lighthouse was six miles north of Shur. In the ancient world, lighthouses had guided ships to safe shores. However, sometime during Urdin's history, the land structure had changed and the only remnant of an ocean was the great river itself. Nevertheless, the lighthouse had served as a guide for numerous Shurite oil caravans in the past, and as John had grown older it had become his refuge as well.

Six months had passed since John had died. Joshua had visited his garden regularly to water his plants. He also spoke with Catonell about keeping the garden fresh. Catonell had worked with John in his garden for many years when she was younger.

Joshua was glad to pass on the responsibility to Catonell. He had become busy with the creation of a new Council. Alongside Stone and the clergy he was working to create a constitution that recognized both state and religion. He was also lobbying for a renewal period of three years, hoping that Stone would eventually develop a surplus of younger Councilmen, consequently disrupting the clergy's majority in the city's ruling body.

Despite progress in creating a new governing structure, Joshua had been discouraged by the lack of vigor around educational reforms. He had pushed for the reintroduction of libraries, but Paris had met his proposal with fierce opposition. Stone had sided with Paris. Joshua was disappointed but he was not surprised. He was becoming increasingly aware of Stone's concerns.

After his last conversation with Stone following the coronation, Joshua had spoken with his pupils. They confirmed that the books were causing a minor stir in some circles in the city. Some of Joshua's students were openly questioning the legitimacy of a king. Joshua asked these students to study more books before proceeding to irrational and potentially detrimental conclusions. Some of his pupils had listened but others had begun meeting separately to discuss the angst that was revived within them by the ink of ancient revolutionaries. Yet Joshua continued his private teachings and, to an extent, Stone reluctantly turned a blind eye.

"Joshua," Stone stood behind him.

Joshua turned from the window.

"Go home," he said. "It's late and we can't do more work here."

Joshua nodded his head. He left the Council Hall just before sunset and went to have dinner with his mother. He arrived before dinner and helped her in the kitchen. After cooking the meal they sat in the courtyard and spoke to each other late into the night. He left her home before midnight and stopped by to see his sister. She was asleep, so he spoke with Mehabiah for a couple of hours. Stone had asked all Council members to take a few days off, and both Joshua and Mehabiah wanted to stay up late.

With the moon halfway across the sky, Joshua left Mehabiah's home and walked through the streets of Shur. As with any weekend night, Joshua came across small pockets of people in ancient Shur gathered around small fires. Some of them played music and some read his books. They hid the books when they first saw him approaching from afar. But when they realized that it was him they smiled.

He stopped by many small gatherings and asked them to temper their readings with rational thought and understanding. He also asked them to balance their knowledge by reading numerous authors with varying viewpoints. He specified Machiavelli and Plato, emphasizing the possibility of the absolute truth lying somewhere in between the ideals of both men. The people nodded as he spoke to them, but he wasn't sure if they really understood his message.

The desecration of religious statues was increasing, and anti-government graffiti was spreading as well. Initially he and the Gatherers had successfully found and removed the problems with a little soap and water. However, the incidents had become too numerous to remedy. Many people he spoke to during the night supported the revolutionary banners graffitied across the city. The effects of a thousand years of governmental and religious control were boiling over within them. Joshua's books had given them a voice and a standard by which they were measuring their lives. They had never known the extent of their condition until they had been exposed to the ancient books.

As he spoke with the people on the street, Joshua wondered if he had distributed books to the masses too soon. Originally, the renaissance had taken root with John educating the Gatherers. He had then expanded his teachings to include some important business families. Regardless, he had always limited his renaissance. However, Joshua had expanded the teachings to include the masses. He had gradually started doing so after Jesus' death. Often he would hand out books to people he had only met once or twice. He wanted them armed even if they didn't understand or know how to use the weapons they held.

Years after Jesus's death, with Stone out of the city performing the three tasks, Joshua had conducted a massive dissemination of literature to the people. The people called it a Reeducation. He had appointed spiritual leaders from within the Gatherers to facilitate the knowledge deposited to the masses. Despite Joshua's efforts to organize his educational curriculum, many pupils often met separately and splinter groups were gradually developing.

He looked up at the sky and realized that dawn was approaching. He excused himself from a group of five men who called themselves the Brotherhood of Knowledge. The people's growing interest and their growing awareness encouraged him. Yet he was worried about the potential harm that could come from his hasty reeducation. He only hoped that Stone would be patient when faced with possible insurrections.

❦   ❦   ❦

"I'm afraid he may do something rash," Joshua said.

"Rash!" his mother replied. "Who's being rash, Joshua?"

"The books are necessary," he said.

"And what about Stone?" she said. "Is he wrong? Will a little patience not help?"

"Everyone always waits," Joshua said. "We think we have more time than we really do."

His mother walked toward the flowers in the left corner of the greenhouse. It was her day to nurture John's garden.

"Have you seen Catonell?"

"A few days ago," he said. "She's getting ready for her wedding."

"That girl," his mother said. "Such a pity. He'd be a softer man if she had stayed with him. He's becoming hard. You can see it in his eyes. Such a terrible burden on a young man."

"She says she's happy," Joshua said.

"She says many things," his mother said. "I never liked her. She was an odd child."

Joshua smiled.

"I think I may be getting myself into trouble," he said.

She listened to him while she watered the plants.

"I may be doing things I shouldn't do," he said.

"Just be careful," she said. "He's a good friend."

Joshua helped his mother with the flowers, after which she went inside John's home to rest. The family had taken over John's home. Joshua would sleep over often to keep the house alive. He walked around the garden and looked at the flowers. The greenhouse was warm and he was sweating. He decided to follow his mother into the house.

A sharp, cool wind greeted him as he entered the house. A piercing head rush followed the sudden shift in climate. His eyes were having trouble focusing as well. The house was darker than he remembered.

"Mother!" he shouted. His voice echoed against the walls. He had never heard an echo in John's house before. His mother didn't respond to him. He looked around the house and realized that the furniture was gone. Then from the side of his eye he thought he saw someone. He turned but only caught a glimpse of a shadow.

"Mother," he said again.

He heard a childish giggle come from the corridor to his left. He turned and once again only saw a shadow whisk by into John's courtyard. He walked down the corridor and into the courtyard. It was dark. He was surprised. It was the middle of the day. He looked up at the sky and could see a few stars. His attention was drawn away from the stars by the same sound he had heard inside the house—the soft giggle of a child. He turned toward the sound and squinted his eyes. A child stood thirty feet from him. He walked toward the child, but the child turned and ran back into the house. Joshua ran after the child, and followed him through John's maze of corridors. He ran faster but could not catch the child. The child turned his head as he ran, laughing and pointing at Joshua. Joshua couldn't tell if it was Manu.

Finally, Joshua succeeded in running the boy into a corner room in the house. There was only one door. The child had shut it behind him. Joshua slowly cracked open the door. The room was dark. He could see nothing. He could hear the child breathing in the far corner. He slowly walked toward the corner and tried to adjust his eyes. He could make out a small figure. He walked closer to it and put his hand out.

He stopped. From the corner and from within the darkness, the face of a beast pounced out at him. Its fangs and yellow eyes were only inches away from Joshua's face and its fiendish growl drowned the silence in the room. Joshua's heart stopped. He fell back in an attempt to escape the entity that had replaced the child in the corner. As he fell, Joshua's head struck the hard floor. He was unconscious.

CHAPTER 23

Prometheus Unbound

So Zamin went after his brother and found him at the gates of Nanak. "Here comes that dreamer," said Zamin to his generals. "Come now let's kill him and throw him into the river. Then we will see what comes of his dreams."

—*El-Theikos*, Chapter 47: The Wars, verses 49–51

It had been a few weeks since Joshua's accident. His head had hurt for days afterward. Strangely enough he had slept well since encountering the creature in John's house. As Joshua walked into the small school he had built at the back of his house, he felt well rested. It was a mud hut with a small water fountain in the center and bookshelves against each wall. During Gatherings, he would hide in the great libraries of Nanak and patiently copy a few books, sometimes completely absorbing them so that he knew the text verbatim. He walked toward the water fountain and washed his hands and his face and then brushed through the books against the mud walls. He picked a book on Greek mythology, and turned to the story of Prometheus and Zeus. He read over the story to make sure it was appropriate for the children, and then sat down behind the water fountain.

When he was alive, John used to read the first story. Joshua felt sad, but then he smiled when he thought of John's animated gestures and preposterous fables. He would flay his arms and swing around the room like a tornado and the children would laugh.

The first children arrived in the later part of the afternoon. He looked at them and thought of Manu. He realized he hadn't seen Manu since the accident. Maybe he had been tired and his mind had been in disarray. He felt better now, and he was glad that the child had disappeared from his dreams and from his reality.

The children looked at him and smiled. Their mothers had their faces covered. Joshua knew that they had come quietly and carefully. No one wanted to antagonize the Elders. But the Shurites trusted Joshua, and so they would bring their children to his school and he would teach them the basic tenets of morality and virtue. As time passed, the children learned a great deal from Joshua. Their mothers, too, were fascinated by the literature of the lost world.

Joshua's goal was to break down the barriers of fear erected in their minds by the religious community in Shur. He wanted these innate restrictions destroyed before rebuilding a new moral structure alongside his young pupils. Together, he hoped, like Plato's philosophers, they would make a journey from the inside of dark caves, where one could see only shadows of truth, toward the bright light of enlightenment. He would gradually compel all of them into a journey of knowledge, far away from the false truths that lay in the dark pits of illusion—a darkness that shrouded the city of Shur. He wanted to free the Shurites from their darkness. He wanted to free them from the confines of unquestioned religious doctrine, accepted archetypes, and ancient paradigms that found their truths in parables, dreams, and fear. He knew that somewhere closer to the mouth of the cave, away from all the darkness, existed a pure truth. He wanted to find it, and he wanted others to come with him.

He looked at the children sitting before him and smiled. "Some day," he thought to himself, as he opened the book and began reading the story of Prometheus, the noblest of gods.

"Prometheus looked down upon the world and saw man braving the bitter cold with raw hides. He felt sad, and decided to visit his brother Zeus. He asked Zeus to give man fire, so that man could protect himself from the winter. But Zeus disagreed. He knew that man could do great things with fire, but his mind was not yet ready to fathom its power. Like Helios's kin on the chariot, man controlling fire would only lead to tragedy. Yet Zeus assured Prometheus that someday, when man had evolved further, he would reconsider the issue.

"Dissatisfied, Prometheus grudgingly agreed and walked away. He constantly looked down at man, and his heart would bleed with each passing death. As the frozen corpses mounted, Prometheus decided to act upon his remorse. One night, while the great Zeus slept, Prometheus trapped a mere thread of Zeus's lightning in a bamboo tube, and descended from Olympus into the dark valleys of earth. He then showed man the thread of lightning from which he created fire. In only a few moments he taught man the uses of fire, and he warned them to use it for good only.

"The next morning Zeus awoke from his slumber and announced his awakening with a loud groan that echoed through the cosmos. He walked to the edge of Olympus and looked down at the world of man. He saw man walking around with fire, cooking food, warming caves, and burning down forests, clearing away foliage and replacing it with small mud huts. Zeus, raged with anger, struck his lightning bolt at the skies, as a great roar arose from Olympus.

"Prometheus was immediately summoned. He walked into Zeus's chamber and confessed his guilt. Zeus loved Prometheus greatly. Together, they had fought and destroyed the Titans, and Prometheus had opened Zeus's life to splendid delicacies such as poetry, writing, and art. Prometheus was, as everyone knew, the noblest of the Gods. Unfortunately he was also the most impetuous and rebellious.

"Zeus pointed out Prometheus's folly. He reminded Prometheus that the feeble minds of men would only harness the destructive forces of fire and ignore its divine elements. But Prometheus told Zeus that the greatest method of acquiring knowledge was by making mistakes and eventually learning from them. Prometheus's retort further infuriated Zeus. Therefore, with a heavy heart, he ordered Prometheus to be seized and bound to a mountaintop, where it always snowed and the wind howled ceaselessly. Prometheus was sentenced to spend an eternity chained to a crag, two vultures hovering above him tearing at his belly and eating his liver. He could not die because he was immortal. But he could suffer. And suffer he did for giving man the gift of fire."

❖   ❖   ❖

The sun was high in the sky and a black hawk hovered overhead, circling the temple. Arjuna, dressed in white robes, entered the temple and walked across the marble floors into a small room on the east wing. Fifteen men sitting around a table greeted him. Stone sat at the head, and Roxanna sat close to him. The rest of the men were younger Councilmen. They were asked to leave as soon as Arjuna walked into the room.

"Another one," Arjuna said, addressing Stone.

"How bad is it?" Stone asked.

"It's the worst."

"Does Joshua know?"

"Not yet," Arjuna said. "We found the statue before he did."

"What does it say?"

"Do you want to see it?"

"No, just tell me what it says."

Arjuna pulled out a piece of paper and read from it.

"'the social compact gives the body politic absolute power over all its members and it is this power under the direction of the general will, bears, as I have said, the name of sovereignty. The government of Stone is not of the body politic," Arjuna said.

"Rousseau," Roxanna sighed.

"And the statue?" Stone asked.

"Completely vandalized," Arjuna replied. "Red paint everywhere. The text runs across Jenut's face and across his body."

"Ignorant," Stone said.

"This is the thirtieth incident," Roxanna said. "And it's getting worse."

"Any news from the royal spies?" Stone asked.

"They've reported small incidents," Arjuna replied. "Only murmurs, around game tables and weekend bonfires. One group wants a plural government with no king. They're only thirty men. And there are other groups as well."

"John told me that Joshua had increased his teachings while the caravan was gone," Stone said.

"Your opposition is still small," Arjuna said. "There's really not much to speak of. And they're not sure what they want. They're reading books by Camus and Jefferson. But their thoughts have not yet formed."

"The mob has strange ways of changing hands," Roxanna said.

"I know," Stone said.

"You've spoken to him about this before," Roxanna said. "Be forceful this time. Joshua needs to understand the consequences of his actions."

"I will."

"Do you think he'll listen?" Arjuna said.

"He will," Stone replied. "He knows what's best."

"And if he doesn't?"

"He'll know," said Stone as he turned his face away from his mother in an attempt to conceal the uncertainty in his eyes.

CHAPTER 24

❀

Friends

Hell hath no fury...

—*El-Theikos*, Chapter 130: Proverbs, verse 89

"Run faster."

"You think I can't?"

It was late at night. Joshua and Stone were running down the street, racing each other back home. Joshua pushed Stone aside and laughed as he edged into the lead. Stone recovered and plunged at Joshua's feet, bringing both men crashing to the ground.

"Cheater," Joshua said laughing, as he pulled his robes together, got back on his feet and continued running. Stone smiled and followed suit. The two men pushed and pulled all the way back to Stone's home.

"You're a mess," Stone's mother said, annoyed at the mud spots on their clothes.

The two men leaned in and hugged Roxanna carefully, so that they didn't ruin her beautiful dress.

"It's Mehabiah's birthday," she said. "Now go upstairs and change into something clean."

"Yes, Mother," Stone said.

"And give Joshua some of your clothes," she said.

"Thank you," said Joshua.

"Grown men acting like children," she said.

Joshua and Stone smiled and snuck upstairs, so that the guests wouldn't see them. Mehabiah was entertaining an eclectic group of people in the back room, wondering where his brother and friend had disappeared to on such an important night.

Joshua and Stone didn't take long. They changed and rushed down, and mixed with the guests.

"You're twenty-seven," Stone said, hugging Mehabiah.

"Let's play Shulag," Joshua said.

Everyone gathered around a table and began playing the board game. The guests soon became rowdy, and Roxanna was glad that everyone was enjoying the party. She noticed Stone had snuck away into a corner. He was looking around at everyone with a soft smile on his face. He reminded her of Proteus. They were both serious men.

Stone looked at Mehabiah and his mind raced back to their childhood. He reflected on the past often. He was glad that he did. His memories had no gaps, and he knew exactly who he was because his progression was neatly lined up in his mind.

He put a mug of water down and walked toward his mother. He gave her a hug and kissed her forehead. She held him tightly.

"My son," she said, "You're a blessing."

A knock on the door interrupted her attention.

"Paris," she said, surprised, as she opened the door and welcomed the elder in to her home.

"It's so good to see you, sister Roxanna," he said.

"Come on in, there is plenty of food, and everyone is playing Shulag in the back room.

"Shulag," he said. "My favorite game. I must join them."

Roxanna escorted Paris into the back room. Paris embraced Stone as he walked by. Stone patted him on the back and asked him about his hip. He had fallen out of his bed during a restless night. Paris told Stone that the hip was healing, but the pain had moved to his leg.

"Old age," Paris said. "A divine curse."

Stone nodded his head. Paris walked into the back room. As much as Joshua disliked Paris's politics, he helped the old man feel comfortable by speaking with him often and cheering him along during the game.

"He's a wonderful boy," Roxanna said. "But he needs patience."

Stone agreed. Joshua's compassion often astounded him.

"And look at that old man," Roxanna said. "It's like he's standing on pins and needles."

As a young boy, Stone had always thought that people grew older and became wiser and compassionate. However, as he looked at Paris, Stone realized that many adults were merely children in aged bodies. They still had the same fears and demons. And they were angry that time had passed and their souls had remained stagnant.

"People should reflect more," Stone said.

"What?" Roxanna asked.

"People should think more."

"They should."

"They need to learn more about themselves."

"You're right."

The game of Shulag had ended. The guests were streaming out. Joshua saw them to the door. Then the family and Joshua cleaned up the mess and sat around the fire.

Stone's mother had prepared cold milk for him, and as he drank it a cool sensation took over his entire body. He was surrounded by loved ones: Sophia, Roxanna, Mehabiah and Joshua. They were truly precious to him. For the first time since the discovery of the scriptures he felt relaxed.

His mother asked if they were interested in a story.

"Yes," they replied together.

Roxanna walked toward a shelf and pulled out a book. It was bound up like the ones Joshua had in his school.

"Is that one of Joshua's?" Stone said.

"Yes," his mother replied.

"Tomorrow we have to talk about these books," Stone said to Joshua.

"What do you mean?" Joshua asked.

"We'll talk tomorrow," Stone replied.

"Is everything alright?" Joshua asked.

"Yes," Stone replied.

"Can we get on with the story?" Mehabiah interrupted.

"Lets see," Roxanna said. "How about Prometheus and Zeus?"

"I read that yesterday, Roxanna," Joshua said.

"Is there anything else in there?"

"Well...how about *The Iliad*?" Roxanna asked.

"I think I'll like that," Joshua replied.

He looked at Sophia, Mehabiah and Stone. They seemed agreeable. Roxanna opened the book and started reading. It was close to dawn when she stopped reading. But by then her audience was fast asleep.

❧   ❧   ❧

Joshua had a theory about Catonell's betrayal. She was afraid of being abandoned.

After a draining day at the Capitol, Stone would come to her, sad or disturbed or even pre-occupied, and she would interpret his demeanor as a lack of interest. She feared that he would wake up one day and realize her worth. "Why does he love me?" she would think.

"Can you give it all up?" she had asked him.

"No."

"For me?"

"I would," he said. "But you would never ask me to."

She had remained silent.

As he spent more time at the Council Hall and the demons of her insecurities multiplied, she decided to destroy their memories and replace them with false ones.

She had started her metamorphosis when they were still together. He had been too busy with the Council and too in love with her to notice. But in her mind, she was gradually convincing herself that their relationship was a regrettable affair. And somehow after desperate hours of repeating the same lies in her head a thousand times over, she believed that she didn't love him anymore.

She had told Joshua about the manner in which Stone had treated her. "He was callous with me," she had said. Joshua didn't believe her. He knew Stone, and Joshua realized that the only callousness in the relationship came from her twisted rehashing of reality.

Joshua had always thought that the only thing worse than a loved one's death was a loved one's betrayal. He never really understood why she had left Stone. Why did she trade in true love for deception? She had had her soul mate in the palm of her hands. But, because she was afraid she woke up one morning and threw it all away.

CHAPTER 25

✿

Books

One day, in the future, we'll have great libraries and great schools and scholars. But that is the luxury of an advanced society, where a stable civilized legislature is in place. We don't have that yet. We must build that before we open people's minds to great radical ideas. With a fair legislature, books will compel people toward civil disobedience. But without a strong legislative foundation, we're bound to find ourselves in anarchy, and possibly revolution.

—*El-Theikos*, Chapter 179: Stone, verse 53

Sand dunes surrounded him. The storm from the night before had added a fresh layer of pure orange sand that remained untouched until Joshua rode through on his black horse. His head was covered, and his nose was red and peeling. He had left Shur early in the morning. He was riding toward John's lighthouse.

The horse scaled a few steep dunes, after which the lighthouse was in clear view. It stood six hundred feet high. The white paint around it glowed under the afternoon sun, creating an exquisite contrast with the orange sand and the clear blue sky.

It grew larger as he came closer. He stopped his horse a few hundred feet away from the lighthouse, and then proceeded on foot. The heat was now making him delirious. He shouldn't have left Shur without provisions. The journey was hazardous.

He walked toward the lighthouse. He wanted to scale it and rest at the top. He wished John was still alive. He needed to talk, but had no one to talk to.

His heart ached, and his lips quivered. He closed his eyes. When he opened them, he found himself standing beside the lighthouse. He looked up and almost fell over. He opened the door. A large, steel spiral staircase led to the summit. He started walking up in circles. He thought he'd never reach the top. When he did, he felt relieved.

He was sitting on the rooftop of the world. He could see the plains of Urdin stretch before his eyes. Both cities were in clear view, and the mountains behind him rose higher and stretched farther than even he could remember.

He closed his eyes again and tried to relax. He tried to take away the pain in his heart but he couldn't. He felt sad, and he winced when he thought about the conversation he had had with Stone earlier in the day. Stone had invoked a temporary royal decree banning books. All households with Nanakite books were asked to turn over their collections to the government so that schools with specific curriculums could be set up in the near future. Most of Joshua's books were taken from him. Even though Stone insisted that the ban was temporary, Joshua didn't react well to the governmental restrictions and the mass bannings. In the past, he had been able to conduct his reeducation because Stone had supported him. Secret gatherings were possible because the clergy had lost leverage. In contrast, Stone was revered, and his grip on the Shurites was strong. His restrictions would be taken more seriously by the Shurites; consequently, crippling Joshua's efforts.

Stone had made the decision after consulting his mother and other important people, all of whom Joshua respected immensely.

An official announcement was being made in the late afternoon. Joshua didn't want to be present at the Council meeting.

He felt sad that he couldn't do anything about Stone's decision. He had tried to change Stone's mind. They had argued for hours in the dark, cold temple, but Stone was adamant. He had alluded to Moses, Christ, Muhammad, and Cassandra—leaders of the ancient world. "The greatest teachers took their time with the multitudes. They didn't reveal the truths immediately. They allowed their pupils to absorb partial truths, so that when the entire truth was revealed, they could accept it without being overwhelmed."

Tired and sad, Joshua drifted into a deep slumber. His dreams were marred with macabre images of his city. The metal foundations of the ancient buildings tore through the walls and grew high into the sky until the city was only a myriad of metal weeds, trapping him within. He saw the face of Manu with long fangs, growling at him, chasing him through the weeds. He wanted to stop and fight but he couldn't. The beast was getting closer, and then it disappeared as Joshua walked out of the metal weeds onto a soft, sunny landscape. The desert surrounded him on all sides. An old man stood behind him. The man smiled. Joshua walked slowly over the sand dunes. Suddenly, dark clouds gathered overhead and snow quickly covered the ground. The snow was pure and cold, and felt good around his feet. He knelt down and touched the snow. A quick flash of lightning tore through the sky. He covered his face. When he opened his eyes he was back at the summit of the lighthouse. The sun had disappeared from the sky. Black clouds had appeared from behind Kalabaash and devoured the horizon. Soon the rain came. He stood up and lifted his head to the heavens.

Another Gathering was upon him. His men had to leave for Nanak in a few hours. The weather was troublesome.

🍁   🍁   🍁

Stone's vision was blurred. The images around him faded into each other, and the sounds muffled into incoherent gibberish. He looked around for a glimpse of Joshua and could not find him. The anger, which he so masterfully concealed, was visible on his brow. He felt helpless. He had hoped Joshua would return for the Council meeting. Boycotting the meeting sent a clear message to the Council. There was a rift between the two sons of Shur.

Paris sat in the pews of the Council Hall with a subtle, wry smile on his face, laughter echoing through the confines of his mind. Ahab looked into his happy eyes and could almost hear him laugh.

CHAPTER 26

❀

Catonell

Love: that reason for all unreasonable actions.

—*El-Theikos*, Chapter 492, Assignation, verse 47

An hour before sunset, Catonell walked into the post office across the Council Hall. She had rushed herself because she knew that the council meeting would adjourn at six o'clock, and she didn't want to run into Stone. However, the building was empty and she was met by a sign indicating that mail services were not provided after five thirty. As Catonell turned around to walk out of the office the tower clock struck six. Instead of exiting the building she hid behind a large shelf next to a window. The bells rang as Councilmen exited the hall. They slowly dispersed, leaving behind an empty courtyard. Stone was the last one to leave. It was dark and quiet around the steps of the hall. He shut the large doors behind him and tried to lock them from the outside. Usually John and Joshua would help him, but on this night he was alone and he couldn't lock the doors with his own strength. He turned away from the door and looked across the street at the post office. Catonell withdrew from the window. She could hear his footsteps on the hard, cobbled road between the hall and the post office. The knob jiggled and the door creaked open. She hid in a dark corner. She closed her eyes and stopped breathing.

"Is anyone here?" he asked. "I need help locking the doors."

He looked around. It was dark. He couldn't see much. He turned around and walked out the door, back toward the hall.

She lifted her head slowly and peeked out of the window. He looked different from the last time she had seen him. His shoulders were broader and his face seemed rougher. She had only heard about the scar that ran across his forehead down through his brow. It made him look older. They had told her that he had aged since returning from the tasks. The caravans had been away for several months and he had braved the harshest regions of Urdin.

He looked worn. She remembered when he would come to her and complain about the things that upset him. He would tell her everything because he could tell no one else. And she would hold his head in her lap, and stroke his hair, slowly, against the grain, as he would doze off in her arms. She would then play with the hair on his chin and he would smile in his sleep.

Half asleep, he would tell her about his life. He would tell her that he didn't want to be king, that he wanted to be with her. He would tell her that he had to change the world, and that the life he lived was not his—it belonged to God. He would tell her that they would meet again in another life, and he would be a commoner, maybe a soldier, and she could love him and he could love her back. He would then ask her if she could love a soldier after loving a king. She laughed.

He would open his eyes and look into hers and know that his life was complete. All of his ills would disappear until he would awaken to another day at the Council. Paris, Ahab, John, Joshua, Proteus, Acrisius, Jenut, Zamin, dead men, living men, myths, cluttering his mind. Destiny forcing his hand. Atlas with the world on his back.

She remembered the first time she had noticed his broad shoulders. They were thirteen, and it was an unusually hot summer. Stone, Joshua, and she had been playing in the sun. Stone took off his shirt. She looked at his muscles. She had never seen them before. She touched him. He turned around and stared at her.

"Don't look at me like that," she said. "Don't look at me like that again."

"Like what?" he asked.

"That stare," she said.

"Well don't touch me again," he said.

He told his mother that Catonell had touched his shoulders. His mother smiled.

The same summer Catonell was growing as well, and Stone stopped spending time with her. He thought she was becoming strange, and so he avoided her. Annoyed, she complained to Stone's mother. Roxanna tried to speak to him.

"She's strange," he said. "And sometimes Joshua and I have to do things together."

Joshua had first introduced them to each other. Joshua and Catonell were six and Stone was seven. Catonell had seen Stone from afar and she thought he was beautiful. She wanted to meet him.

"Come," Joshua said. "I'll introduce you to him."

"No," she said.

"Come with me," Joshua said firmly as he dragged her toward Stone.

Stone was in the school yard. He was surrounded by a group of boys. He stood in the center of them. Joshua split through the boys.

Stone remembered the boys parting before him. Behind them stood a little girl. She smiled and shrugged her shoulders and then waved at him. He put his hand out.

"I'm Stone," he said. "What's your name?"

They started spending time together. The three of them were inseparable. But then Catonell started growing up, and Stone started avoiding her. But that did not last long. One day, he looked at her and smiled. She was surprised. There was something about her that was different. He wasn't sure what, but he knew that he wanted to be with her. As they spent time together, sometimes their hands would touch, sometimes their feet. He would hold her and she would giggle. He would tremble. He kissed her. Her eyes grew wide.

"I'm sorry," he said.

"Do it again," she replied.

And he kissed her again.

He pushed against the bolts but they wouldn't budge.

"Arrrghhh!" he shouted. "Where are you?"

Joshua was still in the lighthouse. He wanted his friend with him. He wanted Catonell with him. Standing in front of the Council Hall, with the entire city in the palm of his hands, Stone felt lonely, and Catonell sat in a dark corner across the street looking at him, sometimes wondering why and sometimes knowing why she had ended everything.

His life didn't belong to him, and it didn't belong to her. It belonged to God.

"Maybe I'll wait for the soldier," she had thought. So one day she told him to go away. But he didn't. She told him to leave her alone because she couldn't love him. Once again he didn't leave. He stayed and he pleaded, and he told her how much he loved her and how he would spend less time away from her. But she had made her decision. So she pushed harder, until one day she told him that he had manipulated her. That she never wanted to kiss him when they were fourteen. That he was stronger than her so she let him. That she never liked it when his rough hands touched her. That she never wanted to make love to him and that she regretted giving herself to him because she had never loved him. She pushed and she pushed until she could feel his heart break by simply looking into his eyes. She stared at him coldly, all along dying on the inside. "I'm lying," the voice in her mind screamed. "I'm lying. Don't go away." But she never spoke the words. She remembered watching him walk away from her, down the stairs and out into the street. She ran to a window to see him. He walked across the street and around a corner. He didn't turn back. And she didn't go after him.

"She betrayed me," he had told Joshua afterward.

"What did she do?" Joshua had asked.

"She told me that she didn't love me."

CHAPTER 27

❁

The Stranger

Every soul hath a good and a bad angel attending to him all his life long.

—*El-Theikos*, Chapter 35: Angels, verse 68

Joshua had told Stone about Manu. Stone was amused by Joshua's obsession with his visions.

"You're insane," Stone had said.

"I hope I am," Joshua had replied.

Manu had been the main topic of conversation the last time they had delved into deep philosophical discourse. Stone was thinking about Joshua's visions as he lay in his bed, staring at the thatched ceiling of his mother's home. He hadn't seen Joshua since the last Council meeting. Joshua had left for a Gathering the day after and was still in Nanak. Stone was still angry with him. He had made himself busy at the Council so that he could forget about his friend. But Paris would not let him forget.

"He's bad for the city," Paris said. "You must understand."

Stone didn't worry much about Paris's feelings, but he did listen to his mother, and Roxanna was becoming weary of Joshua.

"I love him, Stone," Roxanna had said. "But he's making strange choices. He shouldn't be so callous."

Despite his mother's advice, Stone tried to remain objective, but the politician in him would take over and the religious devout within him would further reinforce the fallacy of Joshua's position. Moreover, he could not ignore the populace's insurrection anymore. Joshua's teachings were making the people volatile.

"Why is he so stubborn?" Stone thought to himself as he closed his eyes. His world melted around him, as he gradually slipped into a deep slumber.

A knock awoke him from his sleep. He felt disoriented and confused. He found himself standing in a temple at Jenut's altar. "Where am I?" he thought to himself. He tried to speak but he couldn't.

A cool breeze swept through the dark temple. Someone must have opened the temple door. He turned around and faced the door. He saw no one. "Strange," he thought. He turned back toward the altar. He knelt down and began praying. He felt comfortable in God's temple. He felt safe far away from the evil, unnatural machinations of political intrigues. God was his savior, his passion, his friend…

"…do you think He's listening?" a voice spoke from within the darkness behind him.

He turned around. He stood up.

"Who's there?" Stone asked calmly.

"Do you?"

Stone walked slowly away from the altar.

"Do I what?" Stone asked.

"Do you think He's listening?"

"Where are you?" Stone looked around the temple.

Stone squinted his eyes. He could see a figure in black almost completely concealed behind a pillar. He walked toward the pillar.

"Stop!" the voice said.

Stone stood still. He didn't recognize the figure. He put his hand on his dagger.

"Why should I stop?" Stone asked.

"Or I'll leave."

"What do you want?" Stone asked.

"I think you know."

Stone was silent.

Stone squinted his eyes again, and focused in on the blurred, dark figure behind the black pillar. He could only make out indistinguishable shadows.

"The Chosen One," the voice said. "Is that what they call you?"

"Why do you ask?" Stone inquired.

"Why shouldn't I?"

Stone walked toward the shadows. The figure stepped back and concealed itself completely behind the pillar. Stone approached the pillar and looked behind it. He found no one. He was alone.

"Do you want to talk?" the sharp, deep voice was now coming from the dome in the rotunda. "Or do you want me to leave?"

"Who are you?" Stone asked.

"I am Manu," the voice said. "The one who cuts and measures."

"Manu?" Stone asked. He was confused. Manu was the child in Joshua's dreams.

"Are you afraid?" Manu asked.

"No," Stone replied. He was curious but not afraid.

"Of course you're not," Manu said.

"What do you want?" Stone asked.

"No," Manu replied.

"What?"

"Ask the right question," Manu said.

"Which is?" Stone asked.

"You know it," Manu said.

"I don't," Stone said. "What do you want?"

"Is that the question?" Manu asked.

"Can I see you?" Stone asked.

"Wrong question," Manu answered. "Do you wish to keep talking?"

"I don't know," Stone said.

"I can leave."

"I don't want you to," Stone said.

"Why?"

"I want to keep talking," Stone said.

"Are you curious?" Manu asked.

"About you?"

"Yes."

"The one that cuts and measures…," Stone thought.

"Your friend will know."

"Joshua?" Stone asked.

"Of course," Manu said.

"Why do you appear in our dreams?" Stone said.

"Am I appearing in your dreams?" Manu asked.

"I must be dreaming," Stone said. "What do you want?"

"Does it bother you?" Manu asked.

"What?" Stone asked.

"Sharing with him," Manu said.

Stone remained silent. He knew not to share his deepest thoughts with anyone. His father had taught him to keep the darkest secrets locked away in the darkest corners of one's mind.

"Do you think he's loyal?" Manu asked.

"Yes I do," Stone said.

"You're lying."

"You can believe whatever you want to believe," Stone said.

"You're lying," Manu said.

"I trust him," Stone said.

"Do you want me to leave?" Manu asked.

"You can if you want," Stone said.

"Stop lying."

"Do you want me to lie?" Stone asked.

"The truth."

"Fine then," Stone said. "I trust him."

"He can destroy you," Manu said.

"Can he?" Stone asked back.

"When do you think he will?" Manu asked.

"He won't."

"Does that scare you?" Manu asked.

"Do I scare you?" Stone asked.

Manu chuckled.

Stone stood alone in the silence. He walked the width of the temple floor. He could see no one. He was completely alone. He stood silently for a moment.

"Come out," he said.

"..."

"Come out and show yourself," Stone said.

"..."

"You're surprised, aren't you?" Stone asked.

"..."

"You're afraid?" Stone asked.

"..."

"Are you in control or am I?" Stone asked.

"Ha!" Manu replied.

"Where are you?" Stone asked.

"Everywhere," Manu replied.

"Are you death?" Stone asked.

"You don't know death yet," Manu said. "But you're close."

"We're all close," Stone said. "Where are you now?"

"Does it matter?" Manu replied.

"No, not really."

"Why aren't you scared?" Manu asked.

"I've prepared myself."

"Did you think you'd see me?" Manu asked.

"I've thought about it."

"You are the chosen one," Manu said.

"I believe in God."

"Good."

"Did He send you?" Stone asked.

"I'm smiling."

"Why are you smiling?" Stone asked.

"Because you don't know," Manu replied.

"Then tell me." Stone said.

"You will know," Manu said. "It's a surprise."

"......," Stone was silent.

"I'd be running now if I was you," Manu said.

"I don't run," Stone said with a smile.

"I know," Manu said. "They told me you wouldn't."

"They?"

"The others that cut and measure."

"Have they been watching?" Stone said.

"Your destiny belongs to them," Manu said.

"Are they sure?" Stone asked.

"Unfinished business," Manu said. "Too much of it."

"You're changing the subject," Stone said. "Are you afraid?"

"Of you?" Manu asked.

"Yes."

"I'm smiling."

"I'm sure you are," Stone said.

"I'll ask the question," Manu said.

"What question?"

'The question," Manu said. "You haven't asked the question."

"Am I dreaming?" Stone asked.

"Is that your question?" Manu asked.

"No," Stone said. "I don't know what you want."

"I'll ask the question then?" Manu said.

"Okay."

"What have you lost?"

Stone was silent.

"Nothing."

"Not anything?" Manu asked.

"No."

"You need to think more then," Manu said.

"I've lost nothing," Stone said firmly.

"…and what will you lose?" Manu said.

"Show yourself if you're not afraid," Stone said.

"I need to go now," Manu said.

"Let's talk some more," Stone said. "You don't need to go."

"Oh! Yes, I do."

His disappearance was marked by darkness. Stone could see nothing until he was awoken in the morning.

CHAPTER 28

❀

Brothers

Brothers hath an unbreakable bond, stronger than any force on Earth.

—*El-Theikos*, Chapter 554: Children, verse 98

Stone was six and Mehabiah was three and a half. Mehabiah had been crying all day. He didn't like school much, and his teachers had had their share of his bawling. By late afternoon, they walked into Stone's classroom and left Mehabiah with his brother. Mehabiah walked to his brother's desk and held his hand. Stone slowly slid to the edge of his chair and helped his brother onto the chair. Mehabiah looked around the room at the older children, his feet dangling in the air because he was too small for the wooden chair. He looked at his brother. Stone was reciting the alphabet with the rest of the class. Mehabiah paid close attention to Stone's lips and tried to follow along. He was still holding Stone's hand, and he would only let go late in the afternoon when their parents would pick them up after school. Then he would run to his mother and hug her. This sign of affection was followed by anger. "Why do you leave me here?" he would ask. Proteus would lift him up in the air. He would talk about the values of an education. But Mehabiah would not listen. Then Proteus would tease him and fling him across his shoulder. Mehabiah was always Proteus's baby. Stone walked quietly along behind his parents and brother with his school bag around his shoulders. His brother's coloring utensils were neatly tucked away in the front pocket.

The routine was repeated for almost a year. Mehabiah would cry for the first half of the day and would join his brother for the second half. During break they would always be together, Mehabiah holding tightly onto Stone's hand. "I want to go to the bathroom." "Do you have to?" Stone replied. "Yes." Stone walked his brother to the bathroom but it was too dirty. Mehabiah refused to use it and looked up at his brother again. "I have to go to the bathroom." Stone knew the bathroom was dirty and didn't want his brother to use it either, so he walked down the hall to the principal's office. He knocked on the door. The principal came out and looked at the two boys.

"My brother has to use your bathroom," Stone said.

"You need to go use the children's bathroom," the principal said.

"It's dirty," Stone said. "He has to use yours."

So the principal obliged and let the boys in. Stone took his brother to the bathroom and helped him onto the toilet. When they were done, he helped his brother wash his hands and then the boys returned to their classroom.

He loved his brother dearly. It was half past midnight. The boys were awake and ready for their midnight chores. Roxanna blessed both boys before they left the house. They walked out into the dark of the night. Mehabiah walked in front of Stone, and Stone watched him proudly. He would die for his brother, and he would trust him always. He knew that his brother was a Gatherer and that the Gatherers were getting impatient. Yet Stone always believed that some people should be loved completely. His brother was one of such people. Selfless love. It hurt him to know that Joshua was willing to compromise their friendship in favor of principle.

The brothers walked to the closest temple. The temple was dark. Their footsteps echoed off the marble floors. They walked to the altar and knelt down. Their eyes were closed and they began praying. Both men felt peaceful. They were together with their God, and they could feel his divinity within them, reminding them of their purpose and the need for them to transcend basic human follies.

During their prayers both men would converse with God. They would ask him questions about justice, about the unnecessary pain in the world. They would ask him for answers and for explanations. And God would speak back, encouraging love and patience, because in good time all truths would be unveiled. Mehabiah and Stone were both patient because they trusted their God. He was just and merciful.

Stone waited for Mehabiah to complete his prayers. Once he did, the men walked to a room in the corner of the temple. They picked up two large boxes and walked out of the temple onto the streets of Shur. Their first stop was at Noel's home. Noel was a man in his late eighties. His wife had died four years before, and his son had perished in a skirmish with the Nanakites during a visit to the mountains. Stone and Mehabiah quietly opened the back door of his house and made their way to the kitchen. They pulled out food from the boxes they were carrying. Stone started a fire and began warming the spices. Soon Mehabiah added vegetables to the mix. In a couple of hours the food was ready and an exotic aroma took over the house. Upstairs in his room, Noel, half asleep, could smell the food. He knew the boys were in his kitchen. He felt good, realizing that he would wake up to a warm meal.

Once they were done, Mehabiah and Stone put the food in wooden containers, which they left on Noel's table. After cleaning up the kitchen they snuck out the back door and walked down the street to Mola's house. Mola was a woman in her fifties. She had been divorced three times. Each time, her husband had cheated on her. Yet she wasn't scarred. She was a loving woman, doing good for all her neighbors whenever she could. Stone and Mehabiah placed flowers on her doormat and walked to the next house.

Throughout the night, the two brothers made dozens of visits, cleaning up homes, dropping off repaired shoes and tools; fixing ladders, fireplaces and chairs.

"I'm exhausted," Stone said softly.

It was early and the boys walked down the street toward their home.

"You need to rest more," Mehabiah said. "Take a few days off if you can."

"I'll think about it," Stone said. "Is Joshua still in Nanak?"

"Yes," Mehabiah said. "He should be back by dawn. He'll make it for the next meeting."

"I haven't spoken to him for a while," Stone said.

The sun was slowly rising over the horizon. They were both tired. All they wanted was to return home and sleep. As the brothers quietly walked together, Mehabiah started thinking about the upcoming annual games. The preparation for the games was always extensive and painstaking. The coliseum in the center of the city would need preparation and the best soldiers in Stone's armies would be ready for friendly combat and sparring. Some criminals would also be thrown into the mix for entertainment. As he thought of the games, he could hear the cheering of the crowd. Next he started thinking about Joshua and the Gathering, and the quiet river. But the noises of the crowd didn't stop. He shrugged his thoughts aside and looked at Stone. Stone looked back at him perplexed.

"What is that?" Mehabiah asked, referring to the sounds of commotion that reached them.

"I don't know," Stone said, looking around in search of the source of the sounds. He could hear loud screams and swords clashing against one other in the distance.

The brothers started running. They took a sharp right down Main Street. They spotted a group of men in the distance and ran toward them. As they came closer they noticed that some of the men were members of the Council guard. They were involved in a skirmish outside Hector's home. Stone spotted Hector, who had drawn his sword. Before Stone could stop him, Hector pushed a guard to the ground and swiftly ran his sword through the soldier's chest.

Mehabiah stopped in his tracks.

"Oh, no," he sighed.

CHAPTER 29

❀

River

Give me strength O' Lord, for my death awaits me.

—*El-Theikos*, Chapter 45: Reincarnation, verse 4

The black bridge loomed above the river. Streaks of moonlight shown through the starless sky. A mist had descended upon the city, and a cold breeze blew through Joshua's hair and made the giant bridge squeak and sway. He carried a heavy sack on his back. He wrapped his scarf tightly around his neck and held his hands together as he walked toward the river. Thirty feet away, he could see three men behind the mist. They saw him and waved. He nodded and approached them.

The raft was on the river and ready for the Gatherers. The men remained silent and communicated through gestures. They were all heavyset and worked quickly. Samuel walked over to Joshua and took the sack away from him. He opened it and started, unloading the contents onto the raft. The Gatherers stopped for a moment as Samuel removed six books from the sack. They looked at Joshua. He looked back at each of them, directly into their eyes.

They continued unpacking. In the meantime, Joshua turned away from the men and looked at the glorious city behind him. He suspected he would never visit the city again.

"Joshua," Samuel said.

"Yes."

"The raft is ready."

Joshua turned back toward the men and boarded the raft. They pushed off against the shore and began their journey back to Shur. The heavy white mist limited their vision. They searched for the lights and stayed adrift close to the bridge. Joshua sat down in the back of the raft and looked around him. The black bridge loomed over his left shoulder. It reminded him of a giant gravestone. The raft barely caused ripples as it moved slowly through the silent, dark waters. Joshua dipped a finger in the river. The cold water grasped at his hand. He let his hand hang over the side of the raft. The air was cool and pure. In a few hours the sun would rise. He closed his eyes. A thousand images cluttered his mind. He had been thinking of Catonell and Stone a great deal lately. Stone didn't talk about Catonell anymore. Even though Stone maintained a hard, infallible persona, Joshua knew that he thought of her often. At times, his face would become sad and he would stare away into the distance and lose himself in memories of her. The melancholy on his face was that of a lover yearning for a different ending, and the smile that followed was that of a realist realizing the limit of all good things.

Joshua wondered if Stone would be the same man had Catonell married him. He wondered if Stone would have lost himself in a romantic's dream, strewn with soul mates and eternal bliss, instead of pursuing political and religious supremacy. Realizing the futility of analyzing alternate life paths, Joshua dismissed the thought from his mind.

His thoughts of Stone were replaced by a deep, numbing headache. He opened his eyes and rubbed his temples. He looked toward the white sack he had been carrying earlier. The books were still lying beside the sack. He began thinking of his argument with Stone. They had left each other on bad terms. They hadn't spoken since.

He didn't like being angry. He didn't like fighting with Stone. It reminded him of his quarrels with Jesus. They would argue for hours, bantering back and forth. He was perplexed by Jesus's lack of logic. Jesus explained everything through passion and spirituality. During school debates, Joshua would expertly lead Jesus into dead ends, and somehow he would find an answer, which satisfied the judges about as much as it dissatisfied Joshua. He had never won a school debate in which Jesus was involved. Jesus' influence and persuasion skills were supernatural. His mother would always say that Jesus could sell sand to a Bedouin in a desert.

Stone was similar, but Stone's charisma was balanced equally by philosophical logic. He could effortlessly explain the existence of God through logic.

During Council meetings, while Stone eloquently built premise after premise followed seamlessly by a logically-derived conclusion, Joshua would simply sit by and smile because he knew that the same logic could be applied to prove the non-existence of God as well.

"God," Joshua thought. He looked up at the stars. "Are we the only ones who know?" He smiled. He wondered why he spoke with God if he didn't believe in him. He knew that he was ultimately speaking to himself, and the closest entity to God was his own mind. He controlled his world, he willed it into action, and he could destroy it by simply jumping off the raft and allowing himself to drown.

He wasn't sure why he cared about the city or about knowledge, or about finding answers if he didn't believe in God. As the years passed he leaned ever more closely to the cliffs of nihilism. His search for the ultimate truth had unearthed a myriad of questions, and a refutation of nothingness was nowhere in sight. He suspected and sometimes feared that the truth—the light at the mouth of the cave—would essentially validate John's theories of chaos and disorder. Yet, deep in his core he secretly hoped for the complete destruction of nihilism: a truth without God. And thus he kept reading voraciously, unmasking theories, opening doors that led to even more doors, and sometimes to long winding paths with no beginnings and no ends.

Even as a child he had felt the absence of God, and after years of reading books and people, he suspected that religion had been created because a purposeless life seemed too morbid an idea. He didn't blame people for creating God. After all, what else was there to do? Man was born without a purpose. He shouted out to the heavens and nobody answered. And instead of trembling at the echo of his own voice, he stood up, shook his fists at the sky, and shouted "I'll create a purpose...watch me while I create a purpose." And he did. He created God, religion, and civilization, and he allowed himself to live in peace. Maybe life was ultimately as trivial as a group of people playing a board game on a warm Sunday afternoon, pretending like everything really mattered.

John had told him that only a few strong minds can deal with the possibility of nothingness. A life without purpose would create utter chaos in the minds of simpler people. They needed their morning tea and their afternoon walk and their evening prayer.

He wondered if Paris was one of such men. He wondered if Paris really believed in God, or if he leveraged the power of God to promote his own ideals. He also wondered if Stone believed in God. He dismissed the idea from his mind. He didn't like questioning Stone's intentions. Stone had always proclaimed a strong faith in a higher being. His entire family had always been religious. Yet Joshua had always been afraid that Stone's religion would steer him away from a radical enlightened revolution. He knew that Stone's father had abandoned John in favor of religious devotion, and deep in his heart he knew that Stone would do the same to him. Like Proteus, he wouldn't mean it, and like Proteus he'd be right in his own way. But that "way" would not lead to an enlightened Shur. Joshua had waited too long. He had diffused too many revolutions in favor of discretion, and he didn't want to be discreet anymore.

Joshua smiled with amusement when he realized that Stone and Paris believed in the same God yet maintained two completely different lives and sets of morals.

The raft was getting closer to Shur. He could now see Shur's buildings behind the thick mist. The city looked different to him.

CHAPTER 30

❀

Council Meeting

Strife from silence, strife from hatred, strife from misunder-
standing, strife from deception.

—*El-Theikos*, Chapter 104: Commune, verse 76

Joshua had noticed them in the streets. The Council guards were everywhere.
As he ascended the steps of the Council Hall he wondered why the guards were
all over the city.

A few guards stood atop the Council dome, which rose into the starlit sky.
The white pillars raised it majestically closer to the full moon, which floated
upon scattered, thin clouds. The grand steps that led to the entrance of the
building had originally been built so that emperors of the ancient world could
ride their elephants to the doorway. Joshua had never seen an elephant before,
but he knew what one looked like. He had always wanted to see an elephant.
He wondered if John had ever gone far enough to encounter the strange animal.

"Councilman Joshua," a young man said, greeting Joshua as he walked into
the building.

Joshua nodded his head.

The Councilmen were slowly arriving. Most of them carefully avoided
Joshua, but those who caught his eye smiled tentatively. The city had seemed

strange when his raft had arrived. The streets were silent, and the people were hiding in their homes. But the guards were everywhere.

"Joshua," Mehabiah said from behind.

Joshua looked at him and felt relieved.

"What happened while I was gone, Mehabiah?"

"When did you return?"

"It's been an hour."

"I told them to tell you," Mehabiah said.

"I came straight from the raft."

"There was an accident."

Joshua remained silent and allowed Mehabiah to speak.

"The Council guards caught a man desecrating a statue," Mehabiah said. "The man ran, and the guards followed him to a house in ancient Shur. Inside the house, the guards found fourteen other people. They were a part of a teaching group. The house was full of books. Many of them were from your library. The guards asked for the books, and the men refused to give them up. They drew their swords. They fought. Six of them escaped. Eight died. Two guards were spared."

"Whose house?"

"Hector."

"Were they all Gatherers?"

"Yes."

"And the man desecrating the statue?"

"A commoner," Mehabiah said. "Not a Gatherer."

"Why did he run to Hector's house?'

"He was a friend of Hector."

"When did this happen?"

"At dawn," Mehabiah said. "The Council guards have been all over the city."

"I had a few books at my house," Joshua said.

"They're probably still there," Mehabiah said. "But hide them."

"What's going to happen to Hector?" Joshua said.

"I don't know."

"And Stone?"

"He wanted to talk to you but you were gone. Everyone agrees, Joshua."

"About what?"

"The ban must be made more severe, until the people settle down."

"The people are not restless," Joshua asked. "And how can you make the ban more severe than it already is?"

"Council guards will keep a closer watch," Mehabiah said. "The ban is no longer temporary. Stone has removed an end date from the ban. We're going to discuss future plans at this Council meeting."

"Do you know what the plans are?"

"No."

"I have to see Stone."

"He's already inside," Mehabiah said. "The meeting should start in a few minutes.

"I have to talk to him," Joshua said again, as he quickly walked into the Council Hall and made his way into the General Assembly.

CHAPTER 31

❀

Joshua

Be the one who speaks against evil.

—*El-Theikos*, Chapter 89: The Priests, verse 66

"Just go along with it," Stone said.

"With what?" Joshua asked.

"With the meeting," Stone said.

"What's going on?"

"Don't say anything," Stone said. "I tried to find you. Just don't say anything. Stay silent."

But he had not stayed silent. During the Council meeting, six decrees for executions were handed out. Joshua knew that the men were Gatherers, and so he stood up and defended them.

"They killed Council guards," Paris had said.

"Who drew the first sword?" Joshua asked.

"Hector did," Paris said. "It's the testimony of a dying guard. Stone was there. And they were defying their king. They were teaching from your books."

The argument continued. Joshua was not satisfied with the proceedings.

"You don't have a case," Mehabiah whispered emphatically to Joshua.

"They're setting up Hector," Joshua replied.

"You don't have a case!" Mehabiah whispered again. "Stone had banned private readings. Sit down!"

But Joshua did not sit down. Instead he stood at the podium and spoke his mind. He pointed at Paris and Ahab and spoke of the poisonous clergy that was slowly eroding away at Shur's spirituality. His closest friends cringed. They had always known, and they had always told him to use discretion. But Joshua didn't have time for discretion. Paris only looked at him and smiled.

After the meeting Stone stood alone on his rooftop and counted the stars. He felt sad because his dreams were fading. He knew that after Jesus' death, Joshua had become impatient. Stone couldn't imagine the pain Joshua must have gone through. He had not been the same since. He was not as calculating. He was too straightforward and too impatient—qualities that made him a liability in politics.

"Lets get rid of the clergy," Joshua had said.

Stone knew that he couldn't. The clergy had anointed him and were now tied into his destiny. He would bring about gradual changes. He would slowly move toward creating schools and libraries, and then he would raise a worthy successor who would do the same. He would also influence younger clergy members toward concepts of enlightenment, knowledge, science, expressionism, and art. He wanted the people of Shur to gradually evolve. He didn't want them thrown into a hurricane of change, which could potentially decimate them. Joshua disagreed with his perspective. His plan would take time, and after Jesus' death Joshua didn't trust time.

"What if you die?" Joshua had asked.

"I won't die."

Joshua had laughed.

"It'll take time," Stone had said.

"I'm getting older, Stone. Dreams and thoughts don't comfort me anymore."

Stone closed his eyes. He wanted to be young again. He wanted to do everything differently. He wanted to meet Catonell for the first time. He wanted to love her again. He felt sad. The years had passed. He had lost Catonell, and now he was losing Joshua.

"They're both so stubborn," he thought to himself.

He shrugged his feelings aside, took a deep breath, and stood up. He thought of his father.

"For a king to do the right thing, he must remove emotions and focus on objectivity."

"Objectivity," Stone thought. "The tragedy of being king."

CHAPTER 32

Time

During the entire course of our lives, our childhood yearns for redemption.

—*El-Theikos*, Chapter 91: The Past, verse 1

Stone had made his decision. Six men were sentenced to die. Joshua knew that the men were all Gatherers and that Paris would torture them before their execution at the upcoming annual games. Paris wanted to know more about the Gatherers. Joshua hoped that his friends would remain silent.

He had voiced his disapproval during the meeting. He had begged for the Council to spare the men. For the first time in his life he had defied Stone in front of the Shurites. He had looked into Stone's eyes, but Stone had only looked right back at him.

Joshua realized that he hadn't played the political game correctly. He had been too straightforward, and now he had potentially lost the support of his best friend.

"There he is," a voice came out of the darkness.

Council guards were approaching him. Stone stood next to them. He walked toward Joshua. The two men sat down at the riverbank. The bridge loomed above them.

They were silent. Stone spoke first.

"Why did you defy me?" Stone said.

"How could I not have?" Joshua replied.

"We can fight in our homes, but not in front of the city," Stone replied. "I needed you by my side."

"Then destroy the Council," Joshua said. "Let's start over."

"That's not feasible," Stone said.

"Why not?"

"You've got a hard head," Stone said. "And you don't believe in God."

"What does that have to do with anything?"

"You're impatient," Stone said. "You don't believe in an afterlife or another power. You think everything has to happen now."

"I've waited all my life for you to become king," Joshua replied.

"I know."

"And when you do, nothing changes," Joshua replied. "And you think I'm impatient. I'm a realist, Stone. You're my last hope. A thousand years, and you're the first leader to even consider educating the people. I can't hope another one like you will come five hundred years after I die."

"Have faith."

"You're making me angry," Joshua said.

"Because I want you to believe in God?" Stone replied.

Joshua grabbed a white bag, which sat next to him and pulled out a book. He flipped through the pages.

"Have you seen these pictures?" Joshua asked angrily.

"I have," Stone replied.

"Where's God in these pictures?"

"He's there," Stone replied. "You just don't see him."

"What do think this man is thinking?" Joshua asked pointing at the picture. "Do you think he cares about God?"

"You don't understand."

"You're right," Joshua replied. "I don't!"

"It's only a book," Stone said. "*Life Magazine's Pictures of the 22nd Century.*"

"It's life."

"You're looking for God in the wrong books, Joshua."

"See this man!" Joshua pointed to a picture. "He's going to have his head removed with a sword. See this picture of a charred baby. Where is He, Stone?"

"I can't answer that," Stone replied.

"Why not?"

"There's a reason for everything,"

"What is it?"

"I'm not sure," Stone said.

"It's a baby, Stone," Joshua replied.

"I can't explain the universe to you, Joshua."

"Why?"

"I don't know!"

The two men stared at each other. They were both angry.

"We're young," Stone said. "We'll figure it out."

"When?" Joshua asked.

"In a few years," Stone said.

"How old are you now?" Joshua asked.

"Ten," Stone replied.

The two boys sat on the edge of the riverbank and threw stones into the water.

"Happy Birthday," Joshua said.

"Thanks," Stone replied. "My father gave me a sword."

"A sword!" Joshua said giddily.

"Yes," Stone replied.

"Wow!" Joshua replied. "Jesus has a sword. They haven't bought me one yet."

"Even Catonell has a sword," Stone said with a smile.

"No, she doesn't!"

"You're the only one without a sword, Joshua," Stone said.

"Shut up!" Joshua said.

"Do you love Catonell?" Stone asked.

"No!" Joshua said emphatically.

"Yes, you do!"

"Go play with your sword."

"My mom says I should keep it away from the baby," Stone said. "He'll cut himself."

"Your brother's stupid."

"No, he isn't," Stone said. "You're stupid."

"Not as stupid as you."

"Go play with your sword," Stone said with a mischievous smile.

"Shut up," Joshua replied.

"I saw John yesterday," Stone said.

"I know," Joshua replied. "He brought books back."

"My father was upset."

"Why?"

"We don't need books," Stone said. "We have <u>El-Theikos</u>."

"My father thinks it's good," Joshua replied.

"Some books," Stone replied. *"But some are the devil's seed."*
"They're not!"
"That's what my father said," Stone said.
"My father said John doesn't believe in God."
"He doesn't?" Stone was shocked.
"That's what he said."
"Do you believe in God?" Stone asked.
"Why do you want to know?"
"The Elders wanted to know."
Joshua was silent.
"Did the Elders send you?" Joshua asked.
"Nobody sends me," Stone replied.
"We can still destroy them."
"I don't want civil war," Stone said.
"The people love you," Joshua said.
"You need to stop Gathering books."
"I can't," Joshua said.
"We'll work everything out properly," Stone said.
"We could've removed them."
"Properly," Stone said.
"What does that mean?" Joshua asked.
"Let them die…in their own time."
"They're going to execute Hector."
"I know."
"He read *Romeo and Juliet*," Joshua said.
"Yes," Stone said.
"That was his crime?" Joshua asked.
"Please, Joshua," Stone said. "Let's do this properly."
"Properly," Joshua said. "You call killing Gatherers proper."
"He broke the law."
"The law!" Joshua scoffed.
"He had books in his house that were banned by his king," Stone said. "And he attacked a Council guard."
"Who drew the first sword?"
"Hector did."
"My father got me a sword yesterday," Joshua said.
"I got mine when I was ten," Stone replied.
"I remember," Joshua said with a smile.

"And Mehabiah cut his lip."
"It's beautiful," Joshua said.
"It is nice," Stone agreed.
"It's five years newer and better than yours," Joshua said with a smile.
"Newer," Stone replied. "Not better."
"Hah!"
"What's in your pocket?" Stone asked.
"Nietzsche," Joshua said.
"Can I see it?"
"Here," Joshua pulled the tiny book out of his pocket and handed it to Stone.
"Is it good?"
"Yes," Joshua replied. "It makes me think. Do you want it?"
"I don't know," Stone replied. "My father…"
"You can read it here," Joshua said.
"How about something else?" Stone asked.
"Like what?"
"A story," Stone said.
"<u>Macbeth</u>!"
"Is it good?"
"Yes!" Joshua said. "You'll love it."
"What's it about?"
"Murder, daggers, swords, betrayal…."
"That's the last thing we need in Shur," Stone said.
"The people have never liked the Elders."
"I know."
"They're looking for guidance," Joshua said.
"We'll take care of everything."
"Will we?" Joshua asked.
"Yes," Stone replied. "You need to be patient."
"One quick revolution," said Joshua.
"Revolutions are never quick!" Stone replied.
"Why can't they be?" Joshua said.
"Do you trust me?"
"Yes," Joshua said.
"You hesitated."
"I said yes," Joshua said.
"Can you be patient?" Stone asked. "Please."
Joshua was silent.

"Please!" Stone said again. "For our dreams, be patient. It won't take long. We'll work everything out. Just don't be rash!"

"How will we work everything out?"

"We need to fix things for now," Stone said. "I'll tell the Elders and the other Councilmen that you were upset. Better yet, I'll tell them that you were rightfully upset because you were supporting a grand old tradition. Jenut's Gatherers. I'll tell everyone that the clergy would do the same if they came under fire, and that you were doing your duty. How does one argue with defending tradition, especially if that tradition belongs to a prophet? They'll listen to me."

Joshua nodded his head.

"So you're willing to be patient?" Stone asked.

Joshua nodded his head again.

"Is that a yes?" Stone asked.

"Yes," Joshua said.

"You really need to think before you do things," Stone said. "I'll pull together a meeting. I do need to ask you a favor."

"What is it?" Joshua asked.

"Can you talk to the Gatherers?" Stone said. "Tell them not to worry. We'll work everything out."

"They're worried," Joshua said. "Gatherers have never been executed before. They're afraid it might get worse. There are many prophecies that haunt us."

"I promise you that the Gatherers will be safe," Stone said.

"I hope so," Joshua said. "I'll speak to them."

"I'm sorry about Hector."

"But it's more tragic if a good person dies," Joshua said. "It hurts more."

"I really liked it."

"I knew you would," Joshua said.

"Two years," Stone said. "I've read all of Shakespeare in two years."

"And you saved the best for last," Joshua said.

"<u>Hamlet</u>," Stone said.

"He should've just done it."

"Thinking never really helps."

"Sometimes it does," Joshua said.

"Thanks for the books," Stone said.

"You can borrow them any time you want," Joshua said.

"I've liked most of them."

"Which one didn't you like?" Joshua asked.

"Nietzsche."

"*Why?*" *Joshua asked.*

"*He doesn't believe in God,*" *Stone said.* "*He doesn't believe in much at all.*"

"*I know.*"

"*He must've been a sad man,*" *Stone said.*

"*Why?*"

"*Because…*" *Stone said.* "*…God makes me happy.*"

"*Some people might not believe in God and still be happy,*" *Joshua said.*

"*No,*" *Stone said.* "*I don't think that's possible. It'd be scary.*"

"*Anything's possible,*" *Joshua said.*

"*It'd still be scary,*" *Stone said.*

"*It probably would be,*" *Joshua agreed.*

"*I wish they allowed books in Shur,*" *Stone said.*

"*So do I,*" *Joshua said.*

"*Not Nietzsche,*" *Stone corrected himself.* "*But the other ones.*"

"*Why not Nietzsche?*"

"*I don't think people are ready for him.*"

"*Why?*" *Joshua asked.*

"*His ideas promote instability.*" *He sounded like his father.*

"*Do you like the Elders?*" *Joshua asked.*

"*Not really,*" *Stone smiled.*

"*We could learn so much if it wasn't for their rules,*" *Joshua said.*

"*We will,*" *Stone said.* "*Books will be made legal when we're on the Council.*"

"*I hope so,*" *Joshua said.*

"*Yes.*"

"*Do you really think we can do that?*" *Joshua asked.*

"*Yes,*" *Stone replied.*

"*But…*"

"*We'll get there.*"

"It's always been my dream," Joshua said.

"It's my dream also," Stone said.

"We'll build great libraries," Joshua said.

"We will," Stone said. "We're so close."

"Do you really think we are?"

"I promise you," Stone said. "We'll get there."

CHAPTER 33

❀

Games

My eyes have seen all this before. And my ears have understood these wars. And my heart has cried for compassion.

—*El-Theikos*, Chapter 259: Brethren, verses 7–9

"How's Joshua?" Roxanna asked.

"No one has seen him for a while," Paris said. "I think he knows."

"He can't."

"I think he may."

"Even Stone doesn't know."

"How many has it been?"

"Six arrested," Roxanna said. "They'll be taken to the games."

"And the rest?"

"Yes," she replied. "Fourteen more will be arrested at the games. Make sure Stone doesn't hear of this."

The temple door opened. They crouched in the corner of the temple. Stone stood at the entrance. He scanned the temple and walked to the altar. He knelt down and prayed. He had been looking for Roxanna.

He lit a candle, kissed the altar, and walked out of the temple.

"Do you think he saw us?" Paris whispered.

"No."

"When are we going to tell him?" Paris asked.

"Not yet."

"He'll be enraged," Paris said.

"Not if I tell him."

"And Joshua?" Paris asked.

"We'll find him."

"Do you have the message?"

"Yes," Roxanna said. "Give it to the announcer. Tell him to make the announcement during the games."

"And Joshua?" Paris asked once again.

"We'll worry about him later," Roxanna said.

❧   ❧   ❧

The crowd was in a frenzy. The horns drowned the already deafening noise. People were standing in the coliseum that rose five hundred feet from the ground, towering into the few clouds that flirted with the blue skies. The women were dressed in their finest clothes and the men carried their swords and wore golden turbans. They spoke with each other about the day's festivities and the fine weather. Then the horns stopped blowing, and the crowd was silent.

The gates of the coliseum were opened and the royal chariots rode through. Six men, chained to the chariots were dragged along the ground. The crowd saw them and cheered.

A voice from the coliseum tower announced the names of the condemned men. The crowd was silent. After the list was announced, the people turned their attention toward the gates once again, in anticipation of Stone's entrance. Stone rode into the coliseum at the helm of a warrior's chariot. The crowd erupted and cheered enthusiastically as he circled the stadium. He stopped his chariot at the front end of the coliseum and then stepped off and walked slowly to the royal box. He was greeted by Roxanna and the rest of the house of Jenut. The people noticed that Joshua was absent.

The games began once Stone waved his hand. First, Hector was released from his shackles. He was given a sword. The chariots left the center of the stadium. Hector stood alone. The crowd was silent.

Joshua sat in the commoner's section with thirteen of his closest friends. They were all Gatherers from different walks of life. He caught Hector's eye. Hector pointed his sword at Joshua and shouted, "For silence!"

Joshua whispered, "For silence."

The crowd noticed Joshua and cheered.

And then from behind Hector a concealed gate opened, and from within the gate a giant animal appeared. Its paws shook the ground and its fangs dragged along the dirt. Its tail wisped around behind it.

Hector turned around. The beast was three times his size. The beast pounced, and Hector slowly moved aside. The beast turned around and pounced again. This time Hector slashed at the beast before he moved out of the way. The beast growled, and the crowd gasped. Hector had hit a main vein. The beast was bleeding. It pounced again, but this time it wrapped its tail around Hector and pinned him to the ground. The women in the crowd picked up their children and covered their eyes as the beast impaled Hector's body with its fangs.

Joshua turned his head down.

"Are we going to watch?" Samuel asked him.

"They attacked Council guards," Joshua replied.

"Is that their only crime?" Samuel asked.

"I spoke with Stone," Joshua said. "They should be punished."

"We're the defenders of justice?"

"This is justice," Joshua said.

"I wonder how long this will last," Mehabiah said softly. He had left the royal box and had come over to Joshua.

"Go back to the royal box, Mehabiah," Joshua said.

"I'm a Gatherer," Mehabiah replied.

"Quiet now, they're bringing in the others."

The five remaining Gatherers were being brought into the coliseum. Like Hector, they stood their ground. On them, the guards unleashed six beasts that summarily devoured the men. Joshua and the Gatherers winced and watched helplessly.

"Mehabiah."

A Council guard had approached the men from behind. Mehabiah turned around.

"Your mother wishes to see you," the guard said.

Mehabiah looked toward Joshua and the Gatherers, nodded his head, and followed the guard to the royal chambers below the coliseum. Joshua was glad that Roxanna had called for Mehabiah.

The bodies in the coliseum were wrapped in white sheets and dragged away into the dungeons. Joshua had had enough of the massacre. He turned around and walked toward the entrance. He thought the executions had ended, but the announcer was back on top of the tower.

"And now for the next executions," he shouted out aloud. "The following men have been caught by the Council guards reading the books of the old sinful world."

He proceeded to announce the names of the thirteen men standing around Joshua. The men stood still in disbelief. Joshua looked over to the royal box but couldn't see Stone. "This can't be," he thought, but then he saw the Council guards walking toward him. "You promised me," he whispered.

He looked at his thirteen friends, and they all looked back at him, waiting for him to act. He had seen the same look in their eyes when they were boys, playing in the fields, riding their hopes on Joshua's shoulders. He closed his eyes for a moment, and he wished that time would stop.

Joshua quickly concealed the look of disbelief on his face. He glanced over to the royal box again. "Where was Stone?"

He took in a deep breath. The crowd around him was fading away into the smoke of the desert heat and a pounding headache had quickly settled in, drowning out the horrific surprise of the mob in the coliseum. All the desert heat was pressing down on him and the warm wind was blasting in his face, and the sun with its dazzling glare was beating against his back.

He felt alone and helpless, and as the guards approached him and as his decision became inevitable, he began thinking of Catonell, and of Stone, and he thought of Jesus, and the death by the river. He thought of his mother and how she had once told him the story of Helios and the mermaid. It was a sad story. Helios had given up the skies for the mermaid he loved. But she had not loved him back. Yet he would return to her every night, and every morning she would send him back to the cursed heavens.

"Cursed heavens," he whispered, as he placed his hand on his sword. He drew it slowly. It gleamed against the blinding glare of the afternoon sun. The Council guards in the distance stopped. The other Gatherers drew their swords also.

Slowly from the crowd, more men walked toward Joshua and stood around him. They all summarily drew their swords, and chanted "Silence." The crowd around Joshua was multiplying.

Paris stood with the clergy. A look of disbelief was stamped on his face.

"I didn't know there were so many," he said.

CHAPTER 34

❀

Judgment

When a country is rebellious it has many rulers, and only a man of knowledge and power can maintain order.

—*El-Theikos*, Chapter 114: Kings, verse 34

In the confidence of their strength and their hands' work, the Gatherers stood tall to the advancing Council guards and did not give way. Holding up high the tanned leather of their shields they moved straight into the guards. Their swords—raised, blazing in the sun, crimson stained—came down upon their opponents who were pushed back against the coliseum wall, where they were swiftly routed. Surrounded by the carnage caused by his men, Joshua turned toward the south entrance of the coliseum and saw more guards entering the compound.

"How many do you think?" Samuel asked.

"They're sending all of them," Joshua said.

Fifteen hundred guards were marching into the coliseum.

"We'll retreat," Joshua shouted out. "I'll take a hundred with me. Samuel, you take the rest. Try to hide somewhere in the city. I'll take my men into the sewer tunnels. We'll take the Shuria tunnel to ancient Shur and we'll hide there. I'll send word."

"Do we have to split up?"

"Yes, we're too many," Joshua said. "We'll get a message to the rest of the Gatherers to go into hiding as well. Now, go! Go!" Joshua shouted to his men.

Joshua's Gatherers rushed toward the north entrance with the guards chasing after them. Thirty Gatherers stopped at the gates and turned to face the guards. They held off the guards for a while as Joshua swiftly led his men through the streets, almost immediately disappearing into the underground sewer systems. The guards, with their lanterns, followed Joshua and chased his men through the tunnels. The Gatherers were gradually out gaining the guards until they reached a fork in the system. One route, Shuria, led to ancient Shur and the other, Kalabaashia led to the mountains.

"What is that sound?" Joshua asked one of the Gatherers next to him.

They could hear guards coming toward them from both directions. Joshua looked into the tunnel that led toward the city and could see a light from a lantern piercing through the darkness. He looked behind and could hear the guards closing in.

"They've blocked Shuria," he said. "We can't go to Ancient Shur."

He waved his men into the tunnel Kalabaashia. Through the tunnel the Gatherers made their way out of the city and emerged from the darkness into the bright bloom of the desert sun. They continued running. Standing on the edge of the city on the highest rock, Paris could see a speck in the distance as it disappeared into the Kalabaash Mountains. He smiled, suspecting that he would never see Joshua again.

❦   ❦   ❦

Paris returned to the main temple and found Roxanna.

"Do you know where he is?" Roxanna asked.

"No," Paris replied. "The guards chased them out of the city and lost them in the mountains."

"Two hundred and fifty Gatherers," Roxanna said. "Two hundred and fifty men killed eight hundred Council guards today."

"They're Gatherers," Paris replied.

"Your Council guards are useless," Roxanna said.

"They're serviceable," Paris replied.

"You're an idiot, Paris," she said. "You've never been of any use. Not to Proteus and not to Stone. One thing. I asked for one thing."

Paris beat his cane on the floor, turned around, and walked to the temple window.

"I've seen you pout before," Roxanna said. "It gets you nowhere."

"The guards are serviceable," he said again.

"Massacre," she said. "The king's guards were massacred. And the army loves Joshua. A few more days and he'll have them also. And we…we'll have the Council guards."

"What should we do with him?" Paris asked.

"He made his choice."

"It wasn't much of a choice," Paris said.

"Just find him," Roxanna said. "And find out if Mehabiah is with him."

She signaled for him to leave. Paris turned around and left the temple. Roxanna detested him. She sat down at the altar to think. Her thoughts were interrupted by Stone's deep voice.

"Do you still love him?" he asked.

She turned around and looked at her son.

"Yes," she replied.

"Why did you order the guards to arrest them?" he asked.

"Because you wouldn't have."

"We could've done this differently," he said.

"He was in your way,"

"Now we have a situation on our hands."

"If he decides to return, we could have a civil war on our hands, son," she said.

"I know," Stone replied. "He's strong with the army. It won't be long before he tries to get them. And then they're more than just two hundred Gatherers. Soon, they will join him in the mountains."

"You need to be stronger," she said.

"Tell me how?" he said.

"A king does not allow his subjects to disobey him," she said.

"A dictator does not allow his subjects to disobey him," he said.

"You are God in their eyes," she said. "You need to be infallible."

"I'm God in your eyes, Mother, not theirs."

"God anointed you," she said sternly. "You are chosen. The city needs a king at this time, not a philosopher!"

"Why do you think the city needs a king?" Stone asked.

"Joshua's ideals are admirable," she said. "But the people need to understand the responsibility that comes with knowledge and liberty. They don't yet."

"What do you propose?" Stone asked softly.

His gaze was fixed on her, and she searched his eyes.

"You're a disgusting child!" she shouted at him.

"Why?"

"You mock me!"

"I'm not mocking you," he said.

"You're like that bastard John," she said. "Twisting words…"

"Why am I twisting words?" Stone asked.

"Why don't you say what you came here to say?"

"And what is that, Mother?" he said.

She glared at him.

"I'll destroy anyone who touches you," she said. "Joshua was in your way."

"Mother," he said softly. "You believe Shur needs a strong king?"

"Yes," she said. "Of course I do."

"Do you believe in a king who makes his own decisions?"

She nodded.

"Then let me be king," he said.

"I want you to be king…always," she said.

"Do you?"

"Of course."

"Can I trust you?" he asked.

"I'm your mother!"

"Can I trust you?" he asked again.

"Yes!" she said angrily.

"Will you make a decision behind my back again?" he said firmly.

"You little bastard…" she said with a wry smile on her face. "Just like John. Contemptuous and arrogant."

He turned around and called the guards.

Two Council guards walked into the temple.

"Escort my mother home," he said. "Make sure no one speaks with her along the way. Arjuna is waiting for her."

Roxanna walked toward the guards. She lifted her finger.

"Defy me, and you'll taint my royalty, Mother," he said softly.

She glared at him as the guards quietly escorted her out of the temple.

❦   ❦   ❦

They sat down next to the bridge. Stone's eyes were fixed on Nanak.

"My mother told me everything."

"I've arrested everyone involved with her plan," Arjuna said.

"And the Gatherers?" Stone asked.

"They've fled. They're in the mountains."

"Why did he take them to the mountains?" Stone said. "He should have stayed inside the city."

"I don't blame him," Arjuna said. "I'd do the same."

"How's public opinion?" Stone asked.

"They're confused," Arjuna replied. "And extremely volatile. I feel the tide could go either way. You're king, but they've been Gatherers for a thousand years. I'm also concerned about the army. There were five hundred soldiers in plain clothes at the games, and none of them helped the Council guards."

"I'm not surprised," Stone said. "He's their general. But a few days and we'll have them. Do you think we can find him?"

"It won't be easy," Arjuna said. "We can't find Mehabiah either."

"Did you send the message?"

"Yes," Arjuna said. "We sent a messenger to the mountains earlier. They intercepted the message at the base of Kalabaash. But he probably doesn't trust us. I think if the message goes through Mehabiah we'll have a better chance. Mehabiah can play an important role being in the middle."

"Make sure nothing happens to my brother," Stone said. "I don't blame Joshua. Do you think he knows that I didn't call for the arrest?"

"I'm not sure," Arjuna said. "Word is he's collecting all the Gatherers."

"How many?"

"Safe guess would be a thousand, maybe more."

"Civil war?" Stone asked.

"He might," Arjuna said. "Just to shake things up. They're meeting him in the mountains. He may choose to march on the city. If I were him, I'd come back for the army. Gatherers or not, a thousand men cannot stand up against ten thousand."

"We violated their sanctity."

"They disobeyed their king," Arjuna said.

"I promised Joshua that everything would be okay," Stone said. "That his Gatherers would be safe."

Arjuna was silent.

"What's done is done," Stone said. He hated admitting that there was little he could do to rectify the situation.

"What do we do now?"

"We need the army," Stone said. "And we need the people."

"I agree."

"The scriptures are on our side," Stone said.

"Of course they are."

"I think it's time," Stone said.

"For what?"

"We need a war."

"A war?" Arjuna asked.

Stone stood up and brushed his robes. His eyes were still fixed on Nanak.

CHAPTER 35

✿

Revival

If you do not do what is right, sin is crouching at your door.

—*El-Theikos*, Chapter 19: Leviticus, verse 89

"Let's dance until the morning comes," Stone said.

"But we need to sleep," the woman replied.

"But I want to," Stone said.

"Who do you think of when you kiss me?" the woman asked.

"I think of you," Stone replied.

"No," the woman said. "You kiss me gently. Who do you think of?"

He smiled. He didn't want to bare his soul to her. He wouldn't see her again, and he didn't see the point in it.

She looked into his eyes, held his face and said, "Who hurt you?"

He remained silent. He looked into the woman's eyes and thought of Catonell. She was married now. Joshua said that she still loved him.

"Do you ever feel lonely?" he asked the woman.

"All the time," she turned over to her side. "Do you?"

"No," he said.

"I'm sure you don't," she said. "I'm sure you're always with people."

"Do you know Joshua?"

"I've seen him."

"He's lonely," Stone said.

"Why do you say that?" she asked.

"He doesn't spend time with people," he said.

"Why does that make him lonely?" she asked.

"I need to go," he said. He was thinking of his family, and he wanted to be with them.

"Stay a little longer," she said. "At least until the sun rises."

He agreed and rested his head on her shoulder. She softly stroked his hair. Her hands felt good, and his heart felt warm, and he wished that he loved her.

❧   ❧   ❧

"Do everything in your power to direct the city," John had told him.

Stone folded his clothes and placed them in the closet. He looked through old belongings hidden away in a small box beside his shoes. He found a story Joshua had written for him a few years ago. He had been sad because of Catonell, and Joshua had given him the story. Joshua loved writing, and he was good at it.

"Helios and the Mermaid," Stone whispered.

Every night when the sun set, Stone would think of Helios and he felt happy for him.

Even John had liked the story. John didn't care much for Joshua's writing. He wanted Joshua to read instead. "You're too young to write," he had said. "You're wasting your time."

Stone thought of John and smiled.

"Why did you set it up like this?" Stone mumbled.

John had thought long and hard before he made Joshua a Gatherer. By dividing up the power, he was ensured that at least one of the two boys would prevail. "If one falls off the path, the other will steady the city," he had told Joshua's mother. She didn't like the idea.

"Stone," Roxanna stood at his door.

"Mother," Stone said. He walked toward his mother and held her. She shriveled back and pushed him aside.

"Paris is here," she said coldly.

"You can send him up," Stone said.

She turned around and walked away. Stone continued folding his clothes.

"Stone," Paris said.

Stone turned around.

"Councilman Paris."

"You want the scriptures unveiled?" Paris asked.

Stone nodded his head.

"And the sermons?"

"Thirty years ago, you reminded the Shurites of their God," Stone said.

"It was the right thing to do."

"We need to do it again," Stone said. "The people are losing sight."

"I'll need to prepare sermons," Paris said.

"In every temple," Stone said. "Go to their homes if you have to."

"We will."

"Remind them of their God, and then remind them of their king."

"Absolutely," Paris said.

"And one more thing," Stone said.

Paris leaned in.

"Plant the seeds for a return," Stone said.

"A return?" Paris asked.

"To Nanak," Stone replied. "Mention the covenant. I need you to do this in the next two days."

"But we can't take Nanak without the Gatherers."

"Don't worry about the Gatherers," Stone said.

Paris nodded his head.

"Should we do this now?" Paris asked.

"We have to return sometime," Stone said. "It's God's will. I feel the circumstances now are compelling."

"I agree," Paris said.

"My father trusted you," Stone said. He extended his hand. Paris smiled graciously. After a long time, he felt needed and that felt good.

CHAPTER 36

❀

Darkness

If I forget you, O' Nanak, may my right hand forget its skill, may my tongue cling to the roof of my mouth.

—*El-Theikos*, Chapter 109: Prophecies II, verse 77

He didn't really know where he was going, but he kept walking.

"Do you think we'll ever know?" the boy whispered.

"I don't know," Joshua replied.

"Do you know where we're going?" the boy asked again.

"I'm not sure."

He stopped walking. He was surrounded by darkness. His heart was heavy because he saw no light. The cave seemed like it was closing in around him.

"We're counting on you," the boy said.

"I'm not sure if you should," Joshua replied, squinting his eyes hoping to catch a glimmer of light.

"Do you think we're going the wrong way?" the boy asked.

Joshua was silent.

"I didn't really think of that," he replied.

"We're moving away from the bottom of the cave," the boy said. "What if that's where we're supposed to be?"

"No," Joshua said. "How can that be?"

"Maybe there is no opening," the boy said. "Maybe we're stuck in a cave sealed from both ends."

"No," Joshua said.

"Maybe it's just you," the boy said. "Maybe you're the one who's trapped."

"No."

"Do you think Stone sees darkness?"

"I don't know," Joshua replied.

"Maybe God is the answer."

"He can't be," Joshua said.

"You can't see," the boy said. "How would you know?"

"Let me look," Joshua said.

"What?" the boy asked.

"You're not letting me look," Joshua said reaching out to the darkness with his hands. "Let me think a while."

"What is there to think?" the boy asked.

"If you stopped talking maybe I could think," Joshua said.

"Do you see anything?" the boy asked. "It's so dark. Did you think it would be like this?"

"No."

"Did you think it was going to be easy?" the boy said.

"I wish it was," Joshua said.

"Look around you," the boy said.

"I can't see anything." Joshua said.

"Do you want to wake up?"

"Can I if I want to?" Joshua asked.

"Why don't you?"

"There has to be a way out," Joshua said. "If I don't find it now, I'll never find it."

"Do you know where to look?"

"I'm not sure," Joshua said.

"Then how will you find it?" the boy asked.

"Don't hit me," Joshua said.

"What?" the boy asked.

"Don't hit me," Joshua said again.

"I'm not."

"Who is?" Joshua asked.

"She is," the boy said.

"Who is?" Joshua asked.

"Your mother is," the boy said.

"Mother, not now, I haven't found it yet."

"What are you looking for?" Meena asked.

Joshua shook his head and pulled the sheets down so that he could see his mother. She sat on his bedside.

"What time is it?" he asked.

"Mehabiah told me you were here."

"I won't be here long."

"Do you think it's safe?" Meena asked.

"They won't look for me here," Joshua said.

"You look so weak," Meena held her son's face in her hands and brushed his hair back.

"I'm fine," Joshua said.

"I'm not sure what to say," Meena said.

"You don't have to say anything," Joshua said.

"I haven't seen you in so long," Meena said. "Have you spoken with Stone?"

"No," Joshua said.

"You can still make things better," Meena said.

"I'm not sure," Joshua said.

"I want you to," Meena said. "You must."

"This isn't too bad. It could be worse."

"My son's dreams," Meena said.

"We talked about this," Joshua said. "And I asked you to be strong if things got bad."

"I know," Meena said. "It's difficult. I still think of you as a child. You're supposed to play with your friends, and come in for dinner, and then go to bed…not this."

"Be strong," Joshua said. "I love you very much."

"I know," Meena said.

"I'll be okay."

"Just make peace."

"I don't think he wants to," Joshua said.

"Send him a letter," Meena said.

"I need to get all the Gatherers together," Joshua said. "And then the army."

"Why not just come out and make peace now?"

"Because I'm not sure about much right now," Joshua said. "He promised me safety before. We just have to be patient and wait. He's already sent us a message. It came through the Bedouins. I'm ignoring it. It could've come from anyone. If he sends a message through Mehabiah then we'll meet."

Meena stood up and paced the room.

"I'll go back into hiding soon," Joshua said. "We're in the mountains. I probably won't see you for a while."

"How long?"

"I'm not sure," Joshua said. "I need you to be strong."

"I know," Meena said.

"We need to be strong."

"I'm not going to see you again," she said.

"Of course you are," he replied.

"No, I'm not." she said. "That's why you've come here today."

"That's not true," Joshua said.

"Why martyr yourself?"

"I'm not going to," Joshua said.

"Hush." Meena turned to the door. "Someone's knocking."

Joshua stood up.

"I'll take the back door."

Meena kissed Joshua on the forehead.

"Think," she said. "Not with passion, think with your head."

"I will."

"And use the candle when you walk downstairs," she said. "You'll fall if you walk in the dark."

❧   ❧   ❧

As the sun rose into the dark skies, the Shurite army was awoken by the clergymen. The entire camp was astir with news of Stone's public address.

The soldiers gathered in the barrack courtyard, and Stone stood next to a statue of Jenut a few feet above the men. When the crowd was silent, Stone began speaking.

Much like John, Stone maintained an iron grip on his audience's attention. First he mentioned the divinity and His influence on Shur and the entire universe. He then harked back to the story of Jenut and Zamin, and followed the tale through the covenant and Jenut's eventual demise in exile, and the unfulfilled promise that had been passed down through the generations, from father to son, a responsibility that eventually needed fulfillment. He spoke of time and circumstances, and God's purpose for the people of Shur. He then linked

God's purpose with the lost scriptures, the anointment of a new King, and an eventual fulfillment of Daud's covenant.

By the time Stone spoke of returning to Nanak, he had energized the soldiers to an astonishing level of religious and nationalistic pride; consequently, his plea for a crusade to the Promised Land was met with enthusiasm. The soldiers showed him their support with thunderous applause.

Stone's skills in religious persuasion were anchored by his complete and unfailing faith in God. Paris stood behind Stone and was glad that the clergy had emphasized the covenant during the daily sermons for the last week. He wondered if Joshua knew about the sermons and Stone's plan for a return to Nanak. He also wondered if Stone planned to siege Nanak with or without the Gatherers.

CHAPTER 37

❀

Journeys

And all the answers are within the holy book.

—*El-Theikos*: Chapter 19: Leviticus, verse 60

Stone looked out of the window at the dark clouds hovering above the city. His generals stood behind him. They were gathered around a gigantic table, going through sheets of paper, drawing geometrical shapes on maps with stencils and compasses. They had been laboring in the room for days.

The door behind them opened. They stopped and looked up as Arjuna walked in. They greeted him briefly and returned to the work before them. Arjuna walked toward Stone.

"It's going to storm outside," Arjuna said.

"It'll probably be a bad one," Stone said. "Make sure the people stay in their homes at night."

"I will."

"Have you heard from him?" Stone asked.

"He wants to meet with you," Arjuna said. "Our spies say he's already made up his mind. A compromise on his part doesn't seem to be an option."

"And you're sure."

"Yes," Arjuna said. "He's planning on marching on the city with his Gatherers."

"So he'd prefer civil war over a religious crusade."

"It appears that way."

"Any conditions?"

"He'll support you if the clergy is removed."

"We've known that all along."

"Anything else?"

"He's trying to go for the army," Arjuna said. "If you don't remove the clergy he's going to meet with the generals over the next few days. He wants security."

"I heard he injured himself," Stone said.

"Escaping into the mountains," Arjuna said. "He can barely walk."

Stone was silent. Arjuna waited for him to speak.

"Talk to Paris," Stone said. "Tell him about our plans. Tell him that Joshua will probably be in Shur tonight."

"I will," Arjuna replied.

"And send word to Joshua. Tell him that I'd like to meet him at twelve tonight," Stone said.

"I'll try to find Mehabiah," Arjuna said. "Do you need anything else?"

"No," Stone said. "I'll be fine."

※   ※   ※

He looked around at the other Gatherers as they stretched their arms over the fire, attempting to escape the harsh winter wind of the Kalabaash Mountains.

He felt sad because his truths still eluded him, hidden away in thousands of books passed down from the past. Soon he would meet with Stone and tell him that the Gatherers would not support an invasion of Nanak. Nanak was a bastion of enlightenment. Joshua feared that the priests of Shur would destroy the city's libraries.

"What are you thinking about?" Mehabiah whispered.

"Nothing," Joshua smiled.

Mehabiah nodded his head.

Joshua looked around him and said, "I feel like it's all ending."

"We'll be fine," Mehabiah said.

"I know," Joshua replied. "I just feel like it's ending for me."

"It isn't."

"I haven't done what I thought I was going to do," Joshua said. "I have no answers, Mehabiah. I know nothing."

"That's a start," Mehabiah said.

"I wish I could live forever," Joshua said. "Then maybe we could find something."

"It's supposed to take a while," Mehabiah said. "And one man isn't supposed to do it."

"I'd like to be there when it happens," Joshua said.

"Maybe it will never happen and that will be the end."

"I hope not."

"You never know," Mehabiah smiled.

"Maybe you're right," Joshua said.

"I'm glad we're opposing the invasion," Mehabiah said, even though he realized that his brother could not siege Nanak without the Gatherers. Yet he sided with Joshua. An invasion didn't seem feasible with the city in disarray.

"It must be difficult for you."

Mehabiah nodded his head. He loved both men, and he understood the unfortunate situation between them. Finally, after twenty-six years of friendship, Joshua and Stone found themselves on different sides of an inconsolable divide. Their paths and their goals were neatly lined up on opposite sides, so completely different. Yet Mehabiah held on to hope. They had their differences as children, and they had prevailed. The difference this time was the audience. God was watching and history was taking note.

"He wants to meet tonight in the old city," Mehabiah said. "I'm glad you're meeting him. Samuel and I will go ahead first to make sure it's safe, and then we'll wait for you. If it doesn't look safe we'll turn around and cut you off before you enter the city. Samuel is happy that we're trusting him with this. He's earned it after the games."

"He's a good boy," Joshua said.

"Just make sure to bring someone with you."

"Don't worry," Joshua said. "I'll take the route from the east past the tower clock. It should be safe."

Mehabiah didn't insist. The Gatherers had already argued with Joshua earlier about his safety. But Joshua wanted to go alone. He wanted to trust Stone.

"What will you talk about?"

"I'm going to ask him to remove the clergy," Joshua said. "If he doesn't we'll march on the city. I think he has the army already, but I can still convince them to lay their swords down. Then he'll negotiate. It will be a direct challenge to his power, Mehabiah. Do you feel alright about that?"

"I can't feel completely alright with it," Mehabiah said.

"I understand," Joshua said.

"Bring someone with you," Mehabiah said, changing the subject. "Don't come alone."

"I'll be fine," Joshua said, looking up at the sky. "Look at the clouds."

"Winter storms," Mehabiah said.

CHAPTER 38

❀

1010 YK

The tower clock struck twelve. Joshua's robes were drenched. The sky shook with thunder. The streets were flooded. Tall buildings rose on each side. The cold wind slashed through his wet robes and brought tears to his eyes.

Joshua kept walking.

Mehabiah and Samuel hid themselves in the shadows of a building. They were worried. Joshua was late. They walked out into the furious storm and stared in the direction of the tower.

They stepped back into the shadows.

Joshua was tired. The wound was deep. He kept walking. Lightning had struck a building. He stopped. Manu stood before him. Manu pointed at him, turned around, and ran into a nearby alley. Joshua followed him and disappeared into the darkness.

Mehabiah and Samuel waited patiently. Joshua had told them not to move. They had argued with him the day before. "Bring someone with you." "No, I'll

meet you there." "Bring someone with you." "Don't worry." "What if…" "Don't
worry."

Joshua stood in the alley. Manu had disappeared.

An old wrinkled hand reached out to him from the darkness.

"Come, walk toward me," the old man said.

Joshua walked deeper into the alley.

"Who's there?" Joshua asked.

"Is it you?" the old man asked.

Joshua stopped.

"Welcome home," the old man said.

"I know who you are," he said.

"Of course you do," the old man replied.

Lightning flashed across the sky. There were nine men in the alley. Paris was crouched in front of them, his hands still reaching out to him.

"What do you want?" Joshua asked.

"Do you see him?" Samuel asked.

"No," Mehabiah replied.

Mehabiah was worried.

"Where is he?" Samuel asked.

"This isn't like him," Mehabiah said.

"You're right, let's go."

"No," Mehabiah said. "Be patient."

They waited for a while and then Mehabiah walked out into the street.

"His wound hasn't healed yet," Mehabiah said. "He said he'd come from the east, past the tower clock."

"Are you sure?" Samuel asked.

"Yes."

Samuel nodded. They started running.

The nine men carried a white cloth. Joshua didn't move. Lightening flashed again. They stood around him. He closed his eyes and looked up at the sky. The cold rain fell on his face. They wrapped the cloth tightly around his body.

Mehabiah and Samuel ran desperately down the street. Joshua was never late. "Where was he?" They looked into each alley as they ran by. They slipped and fell, but they kept running. Why had they waited so long?

The first knife tore through Joshua's abdomen. A gush of blood stained the white cloth. Air quickly escaped his lungs. He opened his eyes, but he could see nothing. A purple haze absorbed the world around him. He couldn't breathe. His hands were covered with blood. He could taste it on his lips. He fell to his knees. "Were you chosen?" Paris asked, as the last dagger pierced his heart.

Mehabiah and Samuel heard the thunder and saw the lightning. They prayed for Joshua. They loved him. They kept running. They were tired. They ran faster. They turned into an alley. They found him. Joshua's body was tightly wrapped in a crimson cloth. His lifeless eyes stared blankly at the sky, and a trail of blood flowed away from his body into a nearby drain.

CHAPTER 39

❀

Return

The rain had stopped. The clouds scattered away over the mountains as the sun slowly rose into the red sky. A sweet smell was left hovering in the air as an aftermath of the storm. The air was cool and fresh. Gradually as the night turned to day, Meena awoke from her slumber and walked into the streets. She walked slowly toward the Council building, where thousands of Shurites had congregated waiting for the army to march by. Some of them threw stones at a steel cage that hung from the Council dome. She could barely see the figure entrapped in the cage. He was crouched in a fetal position, his skin further wrinkled by the rain of the past week. She wondered if he was still alive.

"Meena," a friend recognized her.

At the sound of her name many of the Shurites stopped throwing stones at the cage. They turned around and came toward her, each blessing her and her lost sons. The funeral the week before had been grand. Stone had deified Joshua as a beacon of truth, and had promised the Shurites that Joshua's dreams would be realized soon after the war. Mehabiah had asked for Joshua and Jesus' diary. He had read through it briefly. It was strewn with dreams of a new world—a different world. Gradually, he too would add more to it.

The funeral had been followed by a trial. The trial had lasted for only an hour, during which most clergyman had been found guilty for conspiring and committing Joshua's murder. Later in the night, the army and the Gatherers had locked members of the clergy in giant steel cages.

Each cage hung from temple rooftops around the city. Paris's cage hung from the Council dome.

In the week following Joshua's death, Mehabiah was anointed Leader of the Gatherers. He met with the Gatherers about city affairs, specifically about the invasion. The Gatherers were pleased with the swift removal of the clergy and felt reassured by Paris's confession about the incident at the annual games. After days of discussion and debate, the Gatherers voted to support their king. Most of them were comfortable with the decision. They agreed that supporting the invasion would not compromise their faith in Joshua's ideals. After all, the clergy had been dissolved and Joshua's renaissance would continue after the war without religious opposition.

Meena held her tears back. She had promised Joshua that she would be strong. He had prepared her for the events of the last few days. She was old. Sophia was married. Acrisius was dead. John was dead. Most of her friends were dead, and now her sons were dead, too. No one really needed her anymore. She knew that soon she would sleep one night and not wake up again.

She could hear the army approaching the Council building. Stone led the army, and Mehabiah and Arjuna followed closely behind. Stone caught Meena's eye and smiled. She smiled back at him. Mehabiah stopped his horse close to her and bent down and gave her his hand. She kissed him on the forehead.

"Come back safely," she said.

He promised her that he'd try, after which he turned his horse and rode toward Stone. Stone led the army to the river. Thousands of soldiers slowly mounted the large rafts that had been built for the siege. By the time the Nanakites would notice the rafts approaching it would be too late. Long ago the Gatherers had mapped out the city of Nanak. They knew of almost every secret entrance.

"I'm glad they're fighting alongside the army," Arjuna said.

"They know the city," Stone said.

"How long do you think it'll take?" Arjuna asked.

"Not long," Mehabiah replied.

"A raft is stuck," Arjuna said.

He rode off toward the raft and tried to help the soldiers push the raft into the river.

Stone and Mehabiah were left alone a top a hill with a good view of the Shurite army. Mehabiah looked at the mountains to the left and thought about Joshua. Joshua's murder had left him stunned.

"I can't believe they're all gone," Mehabiah said, thinking about Jesus, John, and Joshua.

"I know," Stone replied.

"God bless them," Mehabiah said.

"We'll see them again," Stone said.

"I saw Catonell today," Mehabiah said. "I haven't seen her in years. I miss her. Do you miss her?"

"Not really," Stone said without looking at Mehabiah.

The two brothers didn't say a word for a little while. The wind gently blew at their robes. Mehabiah turned and looked at Stone. His heart was heavy, and he felt empty.

"Do you feel lonely?" he asked.

Stone remained silent. He thought about Mehabiah's question and decided not to answer him. Instead he looked at his army, as it slowly made its way toward Nanak.

0-595-28923-1